A

We have selected some of the novels
of Harlequin's world-famous authors
and combined them in a 3-in-1 Omnibus series.

You get THREE enjoyable, full-length romances,
complete and unabridged,
by the same author,
in ONE deluxe, paperback volume,
every month.

A Great Value!

Almost 600 pages of pure entertainment
for an unbelievably low price,

ONLY $1.95.

A truly "Jumbo" read,
available wherever paperback books are sold.

OTHER

Harlequin Romances

by CHARLOTTE LAMB

1722—FOLLOW A STRANGER
1751—CARNIVAL COAST
1803—A FAMILY AFFAIR

SWEET SANCTUARY

by

CHARLOTTE LAMB

HARLEQUIN BOOKS

TORONTO
WINNIPEG

Original hard cover edition published in 1975
by Mills & Boon Limited

SBN 373-01938-6

Harlequin edition published January 1976

All the characters in this book have no existence outside the imagination of the Author, and have no relation whatsoever to anyone bearing the same name or names. They are not even distantly inspired by any individual known or unknown to the Author, and all the incidents are pure invention.

Printed in Canada

CHAPTER ONE

THE spring sunshine was deceptive. That mild blue sky, the dancing dazzle of light on the station window, the golden sheen of daffodils on the grass bank—they all disguised the bitter wind which nipped at feet and hands with the aggression of December rather than April.

Kate Fox shivered in her shabby camelhair coat, drawing the collar closer to her face, flushing as her glance collided with that of the only other passenger waiting on the platform.

They had already studied each other with the casual interest boredom breeds on such occasions.

He was the executive type, she had decided with a faint flicker of hostility. He was tall, well-groomed, with smooth dark hair and eyes the colour of the wintry grey sea she had last seen yesterday when she was driving away from her home. His expression was an irritating mixture of the sardonic and the curious. His rather attractive mouth had twitched at her scornful scrutiny, and he had openly returned her interest, his brows lifting so slightly that it just might have been accidental, yet somehow leaving her in no doubt that he intended the silent comment. Kate had lifted her chin in defiance and turned her attention elsewhere.

Now, conscious of his opinion of her clothes, she gave him a cold stare. Her old coat was past praying for and should have been discarded ages ago, but all her spare money had been needed for Aunt Agnes. For the last two years of her life the poor darling had been unable to digest anything but the lightest food; gently steamed fish, chicken and eggs, with plenty of fruit and fresh salads. Working part-time, so as to be with her as much as possible, Kate had only just earned enough for their food. Luckily, the house belonged to Aunt Agnes, and their rates were not too high. Kate had not been aware of the slow deterioration in her clothes until after Aunt Anges's death. When she had sold the house, the solicitor had said, she would have sufficient funds to buy herself whatever she needed. It was then that, reading his half-pitying, half-shocked glance, Kate had realised how shabby she had become. She had flushed and changed the subject.

He had touched, too, on the subject of a future career. Apart from working part-time in a pet shop Kate had not been trained for anything other than nursing an invalid. She had gently rejected the solicitor's well-meant suggestions.

"I've already applied for a job," she had told him.

He had looked surprised. "Oh?"

"I answered an advertisement in *The Times*. It's ideal for me, I think—a post as companion to a widow in rural Essex. A love of animals essential, but no housework or cooking needed."

His smooth, well-trained face cracked slightly into a

frown. "It sounds too much like your previous life. You're too young to bury yourself with another old lady in the depths of the country. Why not go up to London, train as a nurse or a secretary, and enjoy your youth?" He had sighed. "It doesn't last for ever, you know."

She had smiled at him. "I like the country. London terrifies me."

"Well, I hope you will reconsider your decision," he had told her.

She had listened to his arguments politely, but had not changed her mind, and was on her way now to her new home. She had thought of it as home ever since her first meeting with her new employer, who had come up to London to interview several applicants.

A tall, very thin woman in a blue trouser-suit, with white hair coiled on top of her head in thick plaits which formed a coronet, Mrs. Butler had impressed her on sight. From beneath thin brows she had flashed a glance at her out of eyes of so vivid a blue that one blinked when they opened wide. Her nose had been high, arched and imperious, her mouth generously wide, her chin obstinate, to say the least.

She was not a woman one could easily forget—eccentric, determined and memorable. Kate had felt sure that if she did take the job, when it was offered, she would never find her life dull. It might be exasperating, even alarming at times, but never dull.

The journey from her old home in Devon had taken so long that she had spent the previous night in

London, horrified by the noise of traffic and the pace of life in a great city.

It was balm to the soul to stand here, on this small country railway station, and hear the birds singing, the wind bending the grass and the eerie singing of the wires overhead.

This was the last stage of her long journey. The little district line train had been overdue for ten minutes. The station porter had seemed cheerfully indifferent to this fact when she enquired, and, accustomed to country ways, she had accepted his excuse.

Her companion was less amenable. He was tackling the porter again, in sharp tones. The porter vanished into some inner sanctum and after some delay returned, looking sulky.

"Seemingly," he began in his slow drawl, "there won't be no down train for an hour or so. Trouble on the line up there somewhere. They say it'll take a bit of a while to clear the line."

The executive type exploded with wrath. The porter shrugged his inability to do anything about the situation.

"If you don't want to wait along here, best you get the bus into town and get one of them hire cars."

The executive type glanced across at Kate, lifting one brow. "May I offer you a lift? You'll have a long wait."

She looked at her heavy suitcase, then at him, doubtfully. The porter nodded at her.

"You'll be all right with the gentleman, miss," he

assured her. "I've seen him on the train now and then."

The other man gave them both an infuriated look, then bent and picked up her suitcase, grunting in surprise at the weight.

"I'm sorry," she said nervously. "It's full of books."

"I thought you must collect rocks," he commented.

"I'll take it," she said, reaching out a hand.

He swung round, gripping her by the elbow. "Come along. I imagine I can manage this weight. I'm not incapable."

She saw that she had offended him, so did not protest further. The porter watched them, grinning, but his grin vanished when her companion gave him one of his hard looks.

They caught a one-decker bus outside the station which dropped them a short walk from a car-hire firm. Half an hour later they were well on their way along narrow country lanes.

"You said you were making for Abbot's Marsh," her companion observed, glancing at her.

Dragging herself back from the trance into which she had fallen while contemplating the gentle unfolding of the leaves on the elms, Kate nodded. "Yes."

He exclaimed in irritation, "You are really the most uncommunicative girl I've ever met! Most females are eager to launch themselves into an ocean of small-talk. You have to be forced into committing yourself to the most minute fragment of conversation."

She stared at him in astonishment. "My father disliked what he called chattering females," she confessed shyly.

He gave her another of his long, shrewd glances. "I see."

What, she wondered, did he see? She had learnt something about him during their time in the car-hire firm. The long form he had had to fill in had sketched in his background. She had read it nervously over his shoulder. His name, she learnt, was Nicholas Adams. Aged thirty-four. Profession: architect. He had given her a cool, dismissive stare when he caught her reading what he wrote, and, flushing, she had then moved away.

These slabs of fact had told her a little about him, but she was not competent to fill in the detail by observation. She merely registered his look of assurance, his successful glaze, and decided that he must be a good architect and an irritating man.

"Have you escaped from a nunnery?" he asked abruptly.

Surprise kept her silent. Then she said, "I beg your pardon?"

He gestured with a brief glance. "Your clothes; your unworldly air. They seemed to add up to some sort of cloistered existence."

"Hardly likely in this day and age," she said coolly.

He smiled, staring straight ahead at the road. "So mind my own business? I get the message. May I ask where you're going? Or is that, too, a purely private matter?"

"I thought we'd agreed that I was going to Abbot's

Marsh?"

"I live there myself," he nodded. "I know everyone in the place. Are you visiting someone?"

"In a sense," she said, deliberately evasive.

He turned to look at her, and met warm brown smiling eyes that teased him gently. A grin broke on his face. The cold grey eyes crinkled charmingly.

"I'm glad you're enjoying yourself," he said, laughing. "I was beginning to think you incapable of humour. My name is Nicholas Adams, as I suspect you noticed when we were in the car-hire office. I'm an architect—my own office is in Malden if you ever consider building a house in Essex."

"I'll remember that," she promised gravely.

He groaned. "Do I have to torture you to find out your name?"

"Kate Fox," she said, smiling.

He paused at a crossroads and looked at her, assessing the sleek brown hair, the colour of beech leaves in autumn; the eyes beneath their fine brows and the gentle, tender pink mouth. She had a sensitive, mobile face, responsive to every mood.

"It suits you," he said. "Short but compact, suggesting quick wits and a certain hidden humour."

"There's no answer to that," she riposted.

He grinned and drove on along a wider road which passed a deserted railway station. Suddenly he braked beside a parked white sports car. The driver, a girl with silvery-white hair coiled on top of her head, stared, then opened her car door and climbed out.

"Nick! What are you doing in that old heap?"

He wound down his window. "Hello, darling! Did you come to meet me?"

"I thought you were coming by train. I've been waiting for ages, but there hasn't been a sight of a train."

"There was some sort of trouble on the line—I hired a car for the day and drove here."

The heavily made-up eyes slid past him and focused sharply on Kate. A lifted eyebrow brought Nick's head up.

"Oh, this young lady was the only other passenger waiting for the train, so I offered her a lift." He sounded indifferent and the other girl's lovely face relaxed. The pale pink lips parted in a cool smile at Kate. The green eyes were unsmiling.

"How lucky for her that you hired a car," she drawled.

Kate flushed at something in the tone.

"Do you mind if I have a private word with my fiancé?" The green eyes dared her to mind. A long white hand touched Nick's arm. "Nick? Come over to my car for a moment. I want to tell you something very important."

He murmured an apology to Kate, his eyes a little angry, but followed the girl obediently. He murmured something to her. Kate, staring in the opposite direction, longed to be elsewhere.

Suddenly the other girl's voice rose sharply. "She ordered me off the land! I told her that it was your estate, not hers, and she just said that if I didn't go she would set the dogs on me!"

Nicholas Adams laughed. "Those mangy hounds? They wouldn't bite a hole in a cushion!"

"You're not taking this seriously, Nick. She's your aunt! She only lives there by your consent. How dare she speak to me like that?"

"She's eccentric," he said soothingly. "She probably didn't know who you were!"

"Oh, yes, she did! Because she said I could wait until she was dead before I made my alterations to the furniture."

He looked down at her, his face taut. "Sylvia, what did you say to her? What did she mean by that? I thought I told you we would take our time over persuading her to leave Sanctuary?"

Kate, shaken, sat up and turned to stare at them. Sanctuary? That was the name of the house in which Mrs. Butler lived! Were they talking about her new employer?

Sylvia was looking sulkily at him. "I saw some fantastic white velvet curtains in London last week. I wanted to check the drawing-room at Sanctuary to see how much I would need."

"After what I said to you?" His tone was incredulous.

The green eyes lifted to him, wide and innocent. "But, darling, I wasn't trying to get her to leave. I only wanted the measurements of the windows. Mother thinks we should start planning the new decorations."

"Mother thinks!" His tone was exasperated.

She wound her long white fingers over his arm,

swaying towards him, the pink mouth raised invitingly. "Darling, don't be cross! I meant no harm! But how long must we wait to get our own home? Is it wrong or unnatural to want to live in our own house? It isn't as if you weren't prepared to help her find a new home!"

"I've bought her one," he said, smiling.

"No!" She looked elated. "Where?"

"I bought Rose Cottage," he said.

Her face fell. "Right at our gates? Oh, darling, is that wise?"

"It may swing her over to our side," he said. "After all, she can hardly claim she's being sent away when the new house is right outside the lodge gate."

"She'll never leave Sanctuary willingly," declared Sylvia. "I saw that today. She's an obstinate old woman and totally selfish."

He sighed. "You don't know her well enough, Sylvia. Wait until you do. Aunt Elaine is really very sweet." He hesitated. "I suppose you won't reconsider having her living with us?"

"Even if I would agree, she wouldn't," Sylvia snapped. "She hates me."

He kissed her. "Nonsense! How could anyone hate you?"

Her lashes fluttered appealingly. The white hands were lifted to touch his dark head, then fell.

"I must go, Sylvia," he said. "I shall have to deliver my passenger. I'll call in at your house before I go home."

"Who is she?" Sylvia asked, looking over at Kate,

who flushed and looked away quickly.

"I don't know," he said. "She's a secretive little creature."

"Mousey," agreed Sylvia. "Those appalling clothes! She looks like a refugee."

"Don't be unkind," he said indulgently. "I think she must be rather poor."

"What's she doing in this district? I've never seen her before and I thought I knew everyone for miles around."

"I think she's visiting some relative. Or perhaps she's got a job. Didn't Colonel Lewis say he was expecting a new housekeeper this week?"

"That girl is far too young for a job like that! She can't be more than eighteen."

He shrugged. "Well, I must go."

Sylvia stood waving as they drove away. Kate stared ahead, every particle of feeling tingling with wrath and wounded pride. There was a roar, a flash of white and the sports car suddenly shot past them, at a fantastic speed. The horn blared. Sylvia waved, laughing, and then was gone.

"Silly girl," murmured Nicholas.

"She'll get killed doing that one day," Kate said coldly. "In narrow country lanes that sort of driving is criminal."

"Thank you, Mr. Justice Fox," Nicholas retorted. "Where can I drop you? We're just coming into Abbot's Marsh."

"You can take me to Sanctuary," she said huskily.

"What?" His head swung. The car lurched violently

and there was an ominous scratching along the side as it ran into the hedge. He swore under his breath and drew back. There was a moment's silence, then he demanded, "Did you say Sanctuary?"

"Yes."

"You're going to Sanctuary?"

She gave him a cold look. "Must you keep repeating the same question? Yes, I am going to Sanctuary."

"But that's my house!"

"I gathered as much from your conversation."

"You didn't know until then?" Then he pulled up and stared at her. "Were you listening to my conversation? Eavesdropping?"

"I was in full view," she pointed out. "If you didn't want me to hear you, you should have kept your voices down. It wasn't my fault that I heard. I would have had to wear ear plugs to avoid hearing every word. Your fiancée has a very penetrating voice."

He glared at her. "There's no need to be catty about Sylvia!"

"I was merely stating a fact."

"I've noticed that other women always dislike her. A girl who looks like that has to get used to being the object of jealousy and spite, I suppose."

"I'm not jealous of her! Nor, I hope, am I spiteful." Kate tried not to sound as chagrined as she felt.

"Why are you going to Sanctuary?" He was staring at her with a sort of incredulous dismay.

"I've got a job there."

"A job?" His voice hardened.

"Do stop repeating everything I say!"

"What sort of job?"

"Companion-secretary," she said smugly. "To Mrs. Butler."

"Aunt Elaine? I knew she was up to something when she went up to London so suddenly. I might have known! And I understand her very well—this is the gauntlet."

"What?" Kate was bewildered.

"You," he said impatiently.

"What about me?"

"You are the gauntlet, of course. Thrown down—defiance. I should have expected it."

"I'm sorry," she said weakly. "I don't understand *what* you're talking about."

"Aunt Elaine has been asked to leave my house because I'm getting married, but she refuses to go. To consolidate her position she has chosen to employ you. You're to be her ally. She feels she needs one. Also the very fact that she has engaged you makes her position somehow stronger, makes her a permanent fixture."

Kate sighed. "Oh, dear, it sounds most unpleasant! Are you going to tell me to go away?"

He looked at her in surprise. "Well, what do you think? You must see that your own position will be untenable! I own Sanctuary. I've allowed Aunt Elaine to live there rent-free for years—she isn't even my aunt, really, just an aunt by marriage. Now I want her to leave, and she's perfectly able to buy her own home. She has a private income—money her husband left. It wasn't much ten years ago, but she hasn't had to use it while she lived with me, and she has quite enough to live on for the rest of her life. She is nearly seventy, after all."

"So old?" Kate was astonished. Then, reproachfully, "And you mean to turn her out of her home at that age? It might kill her!"

"We would never have thought of it if she'd been prepared to accept Sylvia, but from the start she set her face against my marriage. We've been engaged for six months, and Aunt Elaine just will not compromise at all. I meant to have her live with us at first, but she quarrelled with Sylvia on sight. They're like a couple of cats. Life would be intolerable. I've done everything I can to reconcile them."

"Perhaps Sylvia doesn't wish to be reconciled?"

He looked irritably at her. "I don't know why I'm discussing this with you. We might as well drive on to Sanctuary as we've come so far. You can stay the night. You must leave in the morning."

Kate said nothing. He drove on in silence, frowning. The hedge-lined lane gave way suddenly to a rough flint wall. Then they came to a high wooden gate. A row of cats sat along the top, staring down at them.

Kate started in surprise. Seeing her face, Nicholas laughed.

"They belong to Aunt Elaine. Didn't you know? She runs this place as an animal sanctuary. I think the name gave her the idea—it's always been called Sanctuary since the Middle Ages when it was a monastery. The house has been in my family for a hundred years."

They passed through the gate and along a road lined with slender silver birch. The spring sunlight rippled through the new green leaves on the branches. Beyond the drive a sloping green lawn led to a calm ring of silvery water, ringed with young willows, whose slanting newly minted leaves swayed in the breeze. Beneath them glinted the gold of crocus and primrose. Behind stood the house, built of the same grey stone and flint as the encircling wall.

"They built the house from the remains of the monastery in the sixteenth century," Nicholas told her, watching her face with deep interest.

She stared in sheer delight, her mobile features revealing every flicker of thought and emotion.

The house was built on a slight curve, like a drawn bow, and at the south end stood a tower, battlemented, with slit windows on all levels.

"A wealthy nabob built the Gothic tower in the eighteenth century," she was quickly informed. "He dreamed of living in a romantic castle. I had it modernised inside—I live there myself and leave Aunt Elaine the rest of the house. My bedroom is at the top there—that Norman arched window."

Kate looked sideways at him from beneath her lashes. "Did you dream of living in a romantic Gothic castle, too?"

He laughed, flushing. "I loved the tower as a boy—always wanted to sleep there. But it was in a state of decay. It was too dangerous for anyone to go up the stairs. They were crumbling away. I've had them renewed and walled in—I did a lot of the work myself. It's fun working with stone."

Cushions of green moss sprouted on the uneven pink tiles of the roof. Wisteria had been trained along the lower wall. A white-painted dovecot stood on the lawn beside the house, doves cooing on the roof, their soft breasts puffed with satisfied complacency.

"Where are all these animals?" she asked.

Nick pointed to the grass behind the house. "Two acres of good paddock there," he said. She could see several horses, a donkey and some tethered goats grazing on the grass. "None of the horses is worth riding," he said. "They're all in an advanced state of decay. Aunt Elaine only takes in very old horses."

"Poor darlings," said Kate.

"Ye gods! I might have known it!" He looked at her in acute dislike, his eyes accusing. "You're another damned animal-lover!"

"Is that a crime?" She lifted her nose in defiance.

He started to laugh. She looked at him with flashing eyes.

"What's so funny?"

"You looked like a little brown mouse when you did that . . . your nose positively twitched." He flicked it gently with one finger. "All you need is whiskers!"

He drove round the back of the house to some old stables. The stableyard was clean and swept. Stacks of sweet-smelling hay were piled in one stall, but there were no animals here. Nicholas parked the car and climbed out.

"We'll find Aunt Elaine in the garden, no doubt,"

he said.

He called loudly as they walked towards the back of the house. At last a voice replied faintly from behind a waist-high privet hedge. Nicholas led the way to a gap in the hedge, and Kate found herself in a large kitchen garden.

Mrs. Butler was digging vigorously among some cabbages. She wore old brown corduroy trousers and a bright yellow sweater. It seemed unbelievable that she was nearly seventy. Her eyes were so young and bright, her smile as she saw Kate was radiant.

"My dear, you got here! How splendid! You can feed the ducks for me before tea!"

"Aunt Elaine," said Nicholas ominously, "what's all this nonsense about giving this young lady a job?"

"Hello, Nick dear. Have you met Kate? Kate, this is my nephew, and such a kind, generous boy. He has given me a home all these years, just as if I were his mother. His mother was my best friend, you know . . . No, that isn't right. His grandmother? Was it your grandmother, Nick dear?"

"My mother," Nicholas said slowly, on a sigh.

"I loved her so much. When she died I was heartbroken. Nick's father didn't know how to bring up a boy alone, and I was so happy to step into the breach." She kissed his cheek, leaving a long smudge of mud across his face. Kate suppressed a smile, and Nick glared at her. "Take Kate into the house to wash before tea, Nick. You mustn't forget your manners. She's a guest in the house."

"We'll discuss the matter later, then," Nicholas

said. "Don't think I've given in, Aunt. I haven't. I've merely shelved it."

"Of course," said Mrs. Butler vaguely. "Do look at these cabbages. Aren't they splendid? So bushy and well-grown. I've had good luck with them this spring."

Nicholas took Kate by the arm and forcibly marched her towards the house, muttering under his breath. A frown creased his forehead and his eyes were furious.

"What you'll find to do I have no idea," he said. "The house runs itself. Aunt Elaine does the cooking. A woman from the village does the heavy work."

"I thought you'd decided I must go?" Kate kept her tone innocent, but he glared at her.

"You know her—you've seen what it's like arguing with her? She just talks about something else. That's how it is over Sylvia. She's never said a word to me against Sylvia—she just talks about something else whenever the subject comes up. It's like trying to fight fog."

"So it's just Sylvia's word for it that Mrs. Butler hates her? You really have no idea what your aunt thinks?"

He looked grimly at the house. "Oh, I have a very shrewd notion. Aunt Elaine can convey a great deal with her silences."

They entered the house by the back door and Kate found herself in a huge, draughty kitchen. The floor was lined with much-scrubbed pink tiles, worn to a gentle rose colour. A recess held an old kitchen range tiled with old Dutch scenes of blue windmills and little rows of stiff blue tulips. Geraniums lined the windows, their pots cluttering the sills. The Welsh dresser was crammed with plates, some painted with birds and flowers, some in traditional willow-pattern style.

The cups and saucers were a motley collection, gay and colourful, painted with orange nasturtiums, roses or trailing ivy. Despite the shadowy, spider-haunted corners, the high ceiling and ill-fitting doors, the room had a homely, lived-in feeling, which made it more inviting than the most modern, well-equipped kitchen in the world.

Under the scrubbed deal table was a basket full of mewing kittens, and Kate fell to her knees to embrace them in delight. They spilled out over her skirt, mild blue eyes shining, claws scratching gently on her coat.

"Oh, no! Where did she get them from? I never leave this house for a day or two but she manages to smuggle some animal or other into it!"

Kate looked up at Nicholas with angry eyes. "Look at them, the darlings! Don't you like kittens?"

He bent to scratch one behind the ear, and found himself with it on his chest, purring loudly and kneading his shoulder with a curled paw, the minute body shaken with heavenly delight.

Kate watched him. She saw the gentleness of his hands, the smile in his eyes.

"They'll have to go tomorrow," Nicholas sighed despairingly. "You will really all have to go tomorrow."

CHAPTER TWO

WHEN Kate came downstairs the following morning she found the kitchen empty except for the kittens in their basket under the table. A kettle purred on the black range. There was a bowl of fruit in the centre of the table, flanked by a large coffee pot, two cups and a bright yellow egg-cup on a green plate.

"I thought I heard you moving about," said Nicholas, coming into the room behind her. "Aunt Elaine is feeding the animals. Will you make yourself some coffee and boil an egg?"

"Am I late?" She looked in consternation at her watch. It was just eight o'clock.

"We get up very early." He watched her making herself some coffee, putting an egg on to boil, slicing and buttering bread. He was flipping the pages of a newspaper, sipping some coffee which looked half cold.

"I must go," he said, shouldering into a dark jacket, straightening his tie and picking up a bulging brief-case. "I have to drive to Malden by nine."

"Goodbye," she said uncertainly, wondering if she would be gone before he got back. From the way he stood there, looking at her and the kittens with a sort of comic despair, she could tell that his thoughts were somewhat similar.

"Look," he said roughly, "I'm sorry about all this—you must be furious with Aunt Elaine and myself. I suppose you've had a rough deal. What will you do?"

She shrugged, carefully peeling an orange with small, slender fingers that shook slightly.

"I will have to find another job, I imagine," she said flatly, keeping her gaze on the orange.

"Why did you take a job like this in the first place? What did your family think of such a crazy idea?"

"I have no family," she told him in a calm voice. One of the kittens scrambled over the top of the basket, falling with a muffled squeal to the floor, and Nicholas fenced it with his foot, very gently, before bending to pick it up and pop it back among its relatives. Then he put down his briefcase and sat down at the table again, propping his head with his hands in a gesture of wry defeat.

"Tell me about yourself! I might as well know the worst."

"The worst?"

He put out one hand and took a piece of orange. "How can I go off to work now? Come on, out with it."

"There's nothing to tell. I'm an orphan, yes, but that doesn't make me a suitable case for charity. You're an orphan yourself. A lot of people are!"

"Where have you lived until now? An orphanage?"

"With an aunt, who died recently." Her voice was deliberately crisply matter-of-fact. She looked at him as he took the last segment of orange. "I hope you enjoyed that. Shall I peel you another?"

He grinned at her sarcasm. "Sorry." He watched her take the top off the boiled egg. "Here, I'll pour you some coffee before it gets cold." He did so deftly, pouring himself some at the same time.

Kate ate her egg without relish. Nicholas watched her over the top of his cup, his expression unreadable. The sunlight, spilling over the geraniums, glittering on saucepans and cutlery and lying in warm yellow pools on the floor, gave the room a new gaiety. She looked around the kitchen. She wanted to stay in this house very much. There was a warm, caring atmosphere which seemed to enfold everyone, human and animal alike.

She had slept like an angel last night in the sparsely furnished room to which Mrs. Butler had shown her. The bed had been old, with brass bedknobs and a sagging feather mattress into which she had sunk as into a snowdrift, every muscle relaxing on a sigh. Although there was only the minimum of furniture, the home-made patchwork quilt, in faded squares of many colours, and the much washed chintz curtains, had given emphasis to the homely feeling, and in the morning sunshine she had felt eagerly drawn to the room.

"What am I going to do with you?" Nicholas sighed.

"Don't worry," she told him, without a sign of her inner struggle. "I shall have left by tonight. I do see your point of view, you know. If I'd known the real situation here, I would never have come."

"Aunt Elaine has a great deal to answer for!" He gave an exasperated groan. "Look, I must get off to work, but you'd better stay until I get back tonight. We'll sort something out then—I may be able to find you another job where you'll be offered a home." His glance was gentle. "That's what you need—a home."

"I can find myself a job, thank you! And I'm not a stray dog looking for a home. I'm quite capable of looking after myself."

"Oh, obviously," he said drily.

Kate flushed. "Everyone isn't as devious as Mrs. Butler. I shall be more wary when I meet my next employer, and make sure I have all the facts before I make a decision."

"Next time choose a man," he advised her.

She laughed ironically. "Would you really say that they were less devious than a woman? I'm not so certain."

"What do you know about men?" His smile scoffed. "Living alone with an old aunt for years! I was right when I thought you looked as if you'd escaped from a nunnery. That untouched face . . . you could be all of twelve years old in some lights!"

She trembled with anger and hurt pride. "I'm old enough to resent personal remarks, anyway, Mr. Adams!" She turned away to hide her trembling lips.

"Will you stay until tonight?" he asked after a pause.

"No." Her voice was decisive. "I shall leave today."

"Don't be ridiculous! Where could you go? You have no home, no family."

"I shall go to a hotel. Aunt Agnes left me the house. Her solicitor has told me to send any bills to him and he will advance the money."

He took her by the shoulders and spun her round, his grey eyes penetrating.

He was a very attractive man, she thought, as she had thought when she first saw him, but now that she knew him better she saw the laughter lines at the corner of mouth and eye, and the kindness which he had striven to fight down because he knew how it could involve him in yet more problems. I mustn't let him be kind to me, Kate thought. I must be strong myself. He has enough problems already.

"Please, Kate," he said softly, smiling down into her small, obstinate features. "We won't make any rash decisions yet. Stay here today at least, and tomorrow we'll think of something for you."

That smile! she thought. She felt her determination seeping away under the impact of that smile. Weakness invaded her limbs.

He read her thoughts, saw the softening of mouth and eye, and smiled again.

"That's it! I'll see you later, then. I must dash—look after Aunt Elaine and the kittens for me!"

When he had gone the kitchen seemed less sunny. Kate shivered and knelt down to talk to the kittens. Their furry bodies and frantically beating little hearts were comforting as she held them, squirming and tumbling, on her lap.

She washed up and tidied the kitchen, then went out to look for Mrs. Butler. She found her in the paddock with the horses, talking to them in a quiet voice while they stood around her in an amiable way, their heads nodding now and then as though in answer to some question she put to them. They were all very old, but still eager for life, with mild eyes that shone with pleasure as they snuffled up the oats from the old woman's hands.

"Ah, there you are," said Mrs. Butler warmly, turning her head to smile at the girl. "Come and say good morning to Hercules, Pat and Grey Duke. The donkey is Polly, by the way, and a very sweet-tempered creature, my dear."

"And the goats?" smiled Kate.

"Oh, monsters! Eat anything—hats, buttons, shoe buckles . . . keep as far away from them as you can. Except when you're milking Rosy O'Grady."

"Milking . . ." began Kate in astonishment, wondering what her new employer meant.

"The nanny—she gives plenty of milk at the moment, and very good for you, too. I prefer goat's to cow's milk."

"I can't milk a goat!"

"You'll learn." Mrs. Butler was unflappable. She walked back to the house, talking about the various animals, her attitude very clearly intended to convey a belief that Kate would not be leaving.

"Your nephew wants me to go," Kate said at last. "And I really think perhaps I should do as he wishes."

"Why?"

"Well," said Kate, astonished, "he is the owner of the house!"

"I shall be paying your salary. I have my own income."

"All the same . . ."

"All the same nothing." Mrs. Butler took Kate by the arm, and shook her, staring seriously into her face. "My dear, we have to rescue that boy from his doom."

Kate stared, open-mouthed.

"Boy?" She thought of Nicholas; tall, urbane, wearing the polish of prosperity, and had to laugh.

Mrs. Butler stared back at her without amusement. "Don't quibble, child. I practically brought him up. That's how I see him. He thinks I brought you here to stop his marriage . . ."

"Me? How on earth does he think I could do that?" Kate exclaimed in a startled voice.

She was waved to silence. "Don't interrupt! He's right—I'll do anything to make sure he never marries that . . . that creature!"

"But how do I come into it?" Kate was bewildered.

"You don't, of course. Except that your arrival has put another brick into my defensive wall." The blue eyes sparkled. "I may be an old woman, but Sylvia won't find me helpless!"

Looking at her, Kate could believe it. "Do you think you should interfere, though?" She looked at the old woman with doubtful eyes. "Your nephew isn't the boy you called him, you know. He's over thirty and surely capable of making his own choice!"

"He's infatuated!"

"A boy might be, but is Nicholas a boy, Mrs. Butler?" Kate spoke gently. "I think you're perfectly well aware that he's a man . . ."

Grudgingly Mrs. Butler said, "The creature is attractive, I suppose."

"She's beautiful," Kate corrected firmly.

"Beauty is not merely decorative." The old voice was clear and certain. "There is a beauty beyond the outer appearance. Beauty is only skin-deep in Sylvia—underneath it she's ugly, ugly with selfishness and greed."

"Oh, you shouldn't say that," protested Kate.

"It's true. If Nick marries her he'll be miserable for the rest of his life, because he's a warm-hearted, generous boy, and once he discovers what sort of woman he's married, he'll hate her."

"They've been engaged for six months and he's had plenty of time to get to know her pretty well."

"She's far too clever to give herself away. Nick works hard, so he hasn't seen all that much of her. She puts on a pretty show when she's with him—I've seen her."

"He'll never forgive you if he thinks you're trying to make trouble for them."

Mrs. Butler sighed. "Do you think I don't understand that? That's why I'm very careful. I guard my tongue and keep my head." She looked out into the rolling distance, at elm and cloud and far, misty spire. "I love this place, but I would go tomorrow with a light heart if Nick was marrying the right sort of girl, a girl who would love Sanctuary as I do."

"I got the impression that Sylvia is very keen on the house," Kate said softly.

Mrs. Butler snorted contemptuously. "Oh, she wants Sanctuary. I know that. She's an acquisitive little magpie. The estate is valuable, and the house is respected locally. It's old and lovely, and she wants to get her hands on it, tear its heart out, vandalise it—hang new curtains, put in brash new furniture, paint it queer colours, no doubt, and have it brought thoroughly up to date."

"It's natural for her to want to make her own impression on the home she'll live in for the rest of her life," Kate said gently.

"That's just it—it won't be a home, merely a show-piece."

Kate sighed. "All the same, it will have to be as she decides, once she's his wife. I dare say she'll prefer to spend more time in the drawing-room and less in the kitchen, but everyone has their own idea of how to run a house."

"The kitchen is the heart of the house!" Mrs. Butler's voice was fierce, but Kate detected a dampness around the corners of her eyes. Her emotions went deep where Sanctuary was concerned.

Gently, she nodded. "While you live here!"

"Anyone with any feeling for the place would see it at once!" The blue eyes flashed, like a kingfisher's wing, bright and sudden. "You feel it, don't you?"

Kate hesitated. She did not want to be drawn into this war. It was not her war, and she had a premonition that if she allowed herself to enter the battle she would end up as one of the casualties.

"I know you do," Mrs. Butler nodded at her, ignoring her silence. "I'm a good judge of character. Sanctuary is not just any house—it's an inheritance, to be passed on to the next generation. A petty, greedy mind, like Sylvia's, can't grasp that."

Kate suddenly felt sorry for Sylvia. She probably did not realise yet just what she was up against—not the meanness of a jealous, frightened heart, but the wide surge of a great, selfless passion, the boundless obsession of a lover.

"What about Nick?" she asked quietly. "You keep talking about the house. Where does Nick come into this? He is a human being, after all, and human beings mean more than houses, however beautiful."

"Do you think he would be happy with her?" Mrs. Butler scornfully shook her head. "Nick loves Sanctuary, too, you know."

"Perhaps he loves Sylvia more?"

"I don't believe it!"

They walked back to the house in silence. The older woman stumbled once or twice, and Kate took her arm. With a proud gesture her hand was shaken off. Mrs. Butler was a woman of great spirit, she thought, as they entered the house. It would have been a very interesting experience working for her, but she felt impelled to go as soon as possible.

"Do you think you could just do one thing for me?" pleaded Mrs. Butler. "Tidy up my office? I seem to have got myself into a muddle. I've been shelving letters for months, and now I can't put my hand on anything. If you could bring order into chaos I should be most grateful."

"I really ought to go at once," Kate said slowly. "I have to find a hotel."

"Why not stay as my guest for a few days?" Then, seeing the refusal hovering on Kate's lips, she added quickly, "Or one night? Just another night?"

"Well . . ."

Seeing her weaken, the old woman pressed home her advantage at once. "Oh, good. That's really very kind. If you would come along to the office just now I'll show you where to find things."

The office was a small, cold room at the end of the stone passage which ran right through the house on the ground floor. Kate stood in the doorway, looking around at the scarred wooden desk, the metal filing cabinet and wall shelving. Then she laughed. A huge, rough-headed dog lay asleep in the corner beside a pair of muddy wellington boots.

"Punch, what are you doing here?" Mrs. Butler ruffled the dog's orange fur so that he looked like a lion, the hair standing out from his massive head as he studied Kate curiously in his turn, his yellowy-brown eyes bright and steady.

"He's a darling. Is he yours?"

"No, Nick's, although Nick pretends to find him irritating. He found Punch drowning in the marshes years back. Brought him home in his pocket, a puppy no bigger than a tea-cup. Can you believe it? Look at him now, the silly great pudding!"

Punch looked up, head to one side, tongue lolling, much pleased by her remarks. Like all dogs he knew very well when he was the subject of discussion and enjoyed the limelight.

"Does he always sleep in here?"

"No!" Mrs. Butler picked up the muddy boots. "I see what happened—Nick took him for a walk before breakfast, and left his boots in here when he came back. Nick is often absent-minded. Punch stayed to guard the boots." She walked towards the door with them, and the dog followed.

When she returned, Mrs. Butler showed Kate what she wanted her to do. Opening the top drawer of the filing cabinet, she looked in dismay and distaste at the great pile of papers which immediately began to billow upwards.

"Could you sort these out? Put aside the important ones, throw away the rest? Any that should be kept can be filed in here."

Kate nodded. "I'll see what I can do!"

She worked in the office all day. There were piles of letters and documents everywhere, dusty and crumpled, some yellow with age, but gradually she began to whittle the piles down.

They had a simple salad lunch, and Kate immediately got back to work. It was dusk when she finally came to an end. She had opened a window, and the moths began fluttering into the room, attracted by the electric light. They hovered around the lamp, singeing their bodies and powdery wings. The birds were giving a valedictory chorus. The goats bleated plaintively and the twilight air was chilly on her skin.

"Good lord, you have been busy, haven't you?" She looked up with a start to find Nicholas in the doorway. He had changed into an old blue sweater which brightened his grey eyes to blue, and a pair of faded old jeans instead of his creased city trousers His face was flushed with night air, his eyes bright, his hair ruffled by the wind.

She smiled at him, thinking how much these casual clothes suited him.

"Come for a walk!" The words were an order rather than an invitation and he did not wait for a reply, taking her arm firmly and leading her out of the room. The house was redolent of herbs, spices and slowly cooking meat.

"Casserole!" Nicholas nodded towards the kitchen range, as they went out. "Aunt Elaine's speciality—cooks itself." He whistled and dogs shot from all corners. "My aunt is bedding down a newcomer in the stable."

"A horse?"

He laughed and shook his head. "You'll see later," he said. "Come on, you need some fresh air before dinner. It's bad for your health to spend hours indoors without exercise. A walk will give you an appetite."

"I've got one already," she said wryly, but he was already striding off into the dusk with the dogs rushing to and fro around him. One of them halted, came back and solemnly surveyed her, his great head to one side. He offered her a consolatory paw and she was forced to smile.

"Thank you, dog." He was very like Punch, she noticed. When she mentioned it to Nicholas later he smiled.

"That's Patch—Punch is his father."

"And that one?" She looked at the third dog, a spidery object on very thin fluffy legs which had a high, excited yap when it barked.

"No connection—Poppy came to us from a family who were leaving England and couldn't take her with them. Punch and Patch despise her. She's rather a silly animal, actually. I don't blame them."

Did he approve of Sylvia's desire to get rid of all the animals who at present inhabited Sanctuary, she wondered, or was he, for all his expressed irritation, secretly quite happy with them?

The high flint wall which ran around the estate was, she saw, totally enclosing, and the land which lay within it was a considerable area. In the twilight it was hard to see exactly how far the Sanctuary land extended on all sides, but it gave the impression of being a great green park, dotted with trees and the grazing shapes of animals, with the wall appearing and disappearing in the distance.

"You do have a lot of land," she said, gazing around with a fascinated look. "Is it only used for grazing animals?"

"At present, yes," he said slowly. "I would like to throw down the walls and add the park to my farm."

"Farm? You have a farm?"

"Of course." He looked at her with amusement. "Sanctuary is an estate farm—I have a tenant who farms it. His family have always farmed my land. He would dearly love to have the Sanctuary park land, but while Aunt Elaine lives here he's unlikely to get his wish."

"Would he graze sheep or cattle on it?"

"No, this is first-class arable land, or would be if it was released and properly prepared to take wheat or oats. It's flat and fertile, well drained, and poor old James would be in heaven if he got his hands on it. It lies right in the middle of his farm, you see, cuts his land in half. If I gave it back to him he would be able to double the size of his yield."

"But the house? That would mean pulling down the house, surely?"

He shook his head, standing still to point out features of the landscape. "No, see that slope to the lake? We would cut across there, draining the lake, of course, and taking in all that land. Then the house would stand with just a small garden back and front, with a path leading to the main road as it is at present. Most of the park lies in front of the house, luckily."

"Sanctuary would still be ruined," she said sadly, gazing back through a rising mist to the house. It looked warm and inviting, with its yellow squares of light from the windows, and the small curl of white smoke from the kitchen chimney.

Nicholas groaned. "Aunt Elaine certainly found the sort of girl she was looking for! I imagine she had to interview half London before she found you!"

"Well, you need worry no longer. I shall leave tomorrow," she returned with dignity.

"Look," he said, staring down at her, "will you listen to me first? I need your help even more than my aunt does."

"You do?" Kate lifted her head to look at him, her brown eyes serious.

"I'm desperate," he went on, grimacing.

Desperate for love of Sylvia? she wondered. Was that what he meant?

"My fiancée and my aunt are in the middle of an all-out war, and the chief casualty so far has been me! I can't go on living like this, with sniping going on over my head. I've got to force a decision somehow." He bent to smile at her hopefully. "That's where you come in, Kate."

"I don't want to get involved," she said hastily, turning to go.

He caught her by the arm. "Please listen to me," he pleaded, his grey eyes fixed on her face.

She hesitated, feeling angry and alarmed at the same time. Why did she feel so confused and anxious? she asked herself. These people were nothing to her. Let them settle their domestic squabble among themselves. They should not drag outsiders into the affair. It was all childish, anyway. Why couldn't they live together peacefully instead of making all this fuss?

She started to give Nicholas her views, and he listened eagerly, nodding.

"Of course, you're right. So right! That's why you must help me. Only someone from outside could do anything, and you're the perfect person to intervene."

"No," she protested.

"Yes—Aunt Elaine likes you, I saw that. She's really taken to you—been singing your praises ever since you arrived. She would listen to you. You could influence her."

"I'm not talking your aunt into leaving her home," said Kate coldly.

He took her hand and held it between his, looking at her with such a hopeful air that she was tempted to laugh. "I've bought her a cottage just across the road. She could keep some of the animals there. I'll keep the rest at Sanctuary until they die of natural causes. After that, no more animals, of course. But surely she can accept that compromise? It means that she gets some of her own way."

"You do know that she has a dream of making Sanctuary a permanent animal rest home, a sort of old pensioner's home for animals?"

"It's impractical," he said impatiently. "I can't afford to run the house like that."

"She means to leave her own money to support it."

"In my house? She has no right to make such arrangements. She has allowed a natural kindness to become an obsession. I hate to hurt her, but I'm going to marry Sylvia whether Aunt Elaine likes it or not. She can't expect to choose my wife for me." He looked at Kate frankly. "Aunt Elaine will be very much more hurt if this war goes on, you know. You can save her from some of that pain if you agree to my suggestion."

"What exactly do you want me to do?" She spoke in sad resignation, knowing that she was already half committed to caring what happened to these people, and that such care meant action on her part.

"Stay, as she wants you to, and tell her frankly what the alternatives mean. I'm determined, Kate. I have to choose between my aunt and my future wife. The natural choice is obvious, even to my aunt. She'll only be badly hurt if she continues to oppose our marriage. Talk her round, help her to see that my suggestion will work. The animals here will always be cared for, but there must be no more of them."

Kate walked away from him, her shoulders hunched. She was a small, wistful figure, in her old cherry-red sweater and much-washed and patched jeans. From behind she looked rather like a young boy, slender and graceful, except for the soft fall of silky hair.

She turned suddenly, lifting her shoulders in a shrug. "Yes, I'll help," she said on a sigh.

He caught hold of her shoulders, exultant, and smiled down into her face. "Thank you, Kate. I knew you would!" He suddenly hugged her, in a brotherly fashion, his rough cheek grazing hers briefly. Kate felt a shiver of premonition trickle down her spine. At the back of her mind there flickered an image of them both, held together, in the growing dusk, against the backcloth of the fast vanishing green of the parkland. She knew instinctively that that image would be recorded in her memory for the rest of her life, but she was not yet sure quite why.

She drew away from him, pushing at his chest, and he stared at her in surprise, then grinned.

"Sorry, did I alarm you? I wasn't making a pass, you know! Just showing my gratitude."

"Then please show it in another way," she said stiffly.

"Haven't you ever been kissed before?" he asked with great amusement.

"Of course I have—that doesn't mean I want to be kissed by any Tom, Dick or Harry."

"Or Nick, apparently," he said, still in a state of euphoric glee. "And it was only the merest peck, a fraternal embrace!"

"I didn't like it," she said crossly.

"So it seems!" He was suddenly angry and turned away with an offended air, stalking off with the dogs gambolling around him in uncertain mood, watching him anxiously for some sign of their own position in his graces.

Kate trailed after him, feeling very silly. Why, she asked herself furiously, had she made such a ridiculous fuss over nothing? She had never had a serious relationship with anyone, had really very little experience of men. He had startled her by his sudden hug.

The moon was rising. It swam, reflected, in the waters of the lake below the house, a pale crescent half veiled in mist. From the dew-wet grasses of the park rose a pale vaporous mist which hovered, waist-high, especially in the hollow around the lake. The house seemed to float above, standing clearly against the sky, a sturdy, safe outline, promising security.

She caught up with Nicholas and he glanced at her grimly, his face unsmiling in the dusk.

"I'm sorry," she apologised. "I don't know why I was so touchy about such a silly thing."

The cold mask dissolved. He smiled, crinkling eyes and nose in the charming amusement which could make such a difference to his face. "Forget it! Do you know 'Old MacDonald had a farm?' "

She laughed. "Yes, of course."

He began to sing, and she joined in, their voices blending well together. They walked up towards the house, singing loudly, and startling the rooks, on their nests in the elms, sending them cawing in disgust up into the darkening skies.

The door of Sanctuary stood open, sending a shaft of bright gold winging into the dark. Their voices faltered and fell silent as someone emerged.

Nick dropped his arm from around Kate's shoulders.

"What," demanded Sylvia in a voice like splintering ice, "is *she* doing here?"

CHAPTER THREE

"WHAT are *you* doing here?" Nicholas asked Sylvia sternly. "I thought we'd agreed that for the time being you would stay away from Sanctuary?"

"Yes, you talked me into that, didn't you, Nick—and your reasons were so good!" Sylvia's voice was scathing. "But you had a reason you didn't mention, hadn't you?" Her eyes flicked over Kate, the stiletto stab of her hostility visible. "So again—what is she doing here?"

"By pure coincidence she was on her way here," he began, giving her a smile. "My aunt had given her a job."

"A job?" Sylvia's voice was brittle.

"Yes. Odd that we should meet on the way here, wasn't it?"

"Oh, very!" Sylvia's voice was loaded with sarcasm. Nicholas looked at her, one eyebrow lifting in surprise.

"Look here, I don't know what you're implying, but I can assure you that it was strictly a coincidence, Sylvia! Why on earth should I lie to you?" His voice was chilly, and the well-cut mouth stern.

Sylvia shot him a look, and Kate saw her visibly struggle with her temper. The lovely face was turned away from Nicholas for a moment, hiding the conflicting expressions raging in it. Kate watched in stricken fascination. Then the exquisite features relaxed and a smile curved on the pink mouth.

"Oh, Nick!" the other girl sighed, taking his hand in both her own. "I'm sorry, I've been a beast. But your aunt has been putting ideas into my head . . ."

"Ideas? What sort of ideas?"

A pretty shrug. Sylvia looked up at him, lashes fluttering. "I somehow got the impression that this girl was your guest. I didn't know she was an employee!"

Nicholas looked down at her sharply, his grey eyes alert. "You misunderstood Aunt Elaine. We had a difference of opinion over Kate . . ."

"Kate? You seem to have got on intimate terms very rapidly, considering you claim she's a stranger!" Sylvia spat the words at him angrily.

Nicholas's face froze, then softened. "My dear girl, you aren't jealous?" A smile dawned on his face. He looked amused and, Kate suspected, flattered.

Sylvia drew breath to retort, then relaxed again. Coaxingly, she murmured, "Have I any reason to feel jealous? Can you blame me, with your aunt implying things? She isn't frightfully subtle, you know. And I'm only human."

"You silly girl," he murmured, slipping his arms around her and bending his head. She lifted her face, compliant and tender, the silky blonde hair outlining her like a halo.

Kate, hot-cheeked and embarrassed, slid past them into the house.

When Nicholas released her, Sylvia put up a hand to her ruffled hair. "Darling, you take my breath away!" Her eyes were lit with a hot glow as she smiled at him.

Nicholas grinned. "Glad to hear it!" He watched her as she looked at herself in her tiny compact mirror, dabbing at her nose and retouching her lipstick.

"You'll have to get rid of that girl," she said softly. "Your aunt will use her as a weapon against us, you know. After all, it means you have one more displaced person to worry about."

"That was Aunt Elaine's intention," he nodded. "She picked the perfect lame duck, too. An orphan without family or home! I'd have to be a Herod to kick her out into the storm."

Sylvia's face tightened with irritation. "Soft-hearted Nick— how your aunt plays on your generosity."

"I'm being practical this time," he said. "Kate has agreed to stay as my ally. I've turned the tables on Aunt Elaine."

Sylvia looked doubtful. "I shouldn't be too triumphant. Your aunt is a very shrewd manipulator."

"We'll see," he said complacently. "Kate is an honest girl. I think Aunt Elaine may listen to her where she won't to us. Kate has no axe to grind. That will be her strength."

"And because you've let her stay she'll be grateful to you, Nick," said Sylvia slowly. "Now that is clever, darling!"

"Good lord, the last thing I want! Gratitude poisons."

Sylvia laughed. "You are funny, Nick. I hope your little scheme works. The sooner we get married the happier I shall be—people are beginning to talk."

"Talk about what?" His voice was abstracted. She shot him a glance of irritated curiosity.

"You aren't listening to me, darling! What are you thinking about? Don't you care that I'm unhappy?"

He turned back to her, face gentle. "Unhappy, darling? What do you mean?"

"I hate to feel a fool, and that's what I look, being engaged all this time, and no date set for the wedding. I've been showered with catty remarks from other girls." Her lids lowered and she gave him a secretive look. "And I'm getting invitations again."

He looked puzzled. "Invitations?"

"From other men! After we announced our engagement the phone stopped ringing and I didn't get invitations any more. Now I get them again . . . and the implication is obvious. People suspect we'll soon be breaking up."

She watched his face closely, but his expression was enigmatic. The strong nose and chin had a hint of sternness. The mouth was unsmiling, but the eyes remained mild.

"You only have to reject the invitations once or twice, and they'll stop coming," he said softly.

"Perhaps I don't want to," she said defiantly.

He was silent for a second, then he lifted her chin with one long finger, and looked into her face. "You don't mean that, Sylvia. You're upset tonight. I'll drive you home."

"I'll drive myself," she said furiously, her eyes full of disappointment. He watched her disappear into the darkness with a frown.

Kate, meanwhile, had been explaining to Mrs. Butler that she had accepted Nick's offer of a job. "He prefers to employ me himself as the job can only be a temporary one."

The vivid blue eyes probed hers. "What's he up to? This sounds like tactics to me! He means to have you fighting on his side, does he?"

Gently, Kate asked, "Must there be any fighting? Why not accept the situation?"

"I couldn't bear to see that creature mistress of Sanctuary!"

"Couldn't you put Nick first, and forget the house? What's a pile of bricks and mortar beside human happiness?"

"Shrewd, very shrewd," said Nick sardonically, and she spun, flushing.

He sauntered into the room, eyeing his aunt with mockery. "The child has a discerning mind. Well, Aunt Elaine? Answer her!"

"The casserole will be ruined if you don't hurry up," she snapped in return. "Go and wash at once, both of you!"

Nick winked at Kate as they both obeyed, but she found it hard to smile back at him. It seemed so stupid and pointless that two sensible human beings should engage in such warfare over the ownership of a house She felt sympathy for both sides, saw both points of view. How could she stay here, feeling as she did?

She was quite relieved to fall in with the household hours, and go to bed very early, since her walk before dinner had made her sleepy, and after an hour helping Mrs. Butler wash up and tidy the kitchen she was quite ready for her bed.

Next day she helped to feed the horses, laughing as they gently nosed her pockets for sugar or apples. One was slightly lame, a tall, rawboned bay with a white blaze on his forehead and one muddy white sock on his left forefoot.

"He has rheumatism, poor old chap. He always gets it when it's going to rain." Mrs. Butler patted his nose.

Kate looked up incredulously at the clear blue sky. There was not a cloud to be seen.

Mrs. Butler smiled. "Wait and see—Hercules is never wrong!"

Sure enough, in the afternoon the rain began slowly, spitting across the windows before settling down to a steady downpour. It rained for an hour. The horses sheltered down by the thickest cover, a clump of elms which, by some miracle, had escaped elm disease when some of the others on the estate contracted it. Mrs. Butler had already bewailed their fate to Kate, pointing out blackened stumps where once a great elm had raised its boughs to the sky.

When Kate went into the kitchen for tea she found a small, thin woman in a blue overall polishing the tiled floor, her arms vigorously circling. She looked up and smiled as Kate halted in the doorway. "Come on in, love—I'm just finishing."

"Will I spoil your lovely shine?" Kate admired the floor with a smile. "You have brought up a polish on it!"

"A floor is for walking on," said the woman sturdily. "Take no notice of the shine." She stood up. "There, that's done for this week. You must be the secretary. I've heard about you from Mrs. Butler."

"I'm Kate," she smiled. "Kate Fox." She held out her hand and the other woman, wiping her own hand on her overall, shook it.

"I'm Mrs. Pepper. I come in four times a week to do a few hours."

Kate smiled at her. "You must work very hard, then, because I'd noticed how spick and span everything is!"

"Pays a bit of work, does this house," Mrs. Pepper said with pride. "I like to do a job worth doing. I can do my own house in half an hour. Whisk round with the vacuum, flick of the duster, and it's done. But a house like this is a real pleasure to keep nice. You feel you've really done something. Old things always gives me that feeling. I collect them, in a small way."

"Do you mean antiques?" Kate looked at her in astonishment.

The thin face creased with amusement. "Oh, not the expensive kind. I can't afford them. I buy old keepsakes . . . souvenirs. China or glass. I like to have pretty things—and if you go to country auctions you can still pick them up quite cheap now and then."

"What a fascinating hobby!"

"It gives me an interest," Mrs. Pepper agreed.

"Would you like some tea, Mrs. Pepper?" Kate put the kettle on the range. "I'm going to have some."

"I won't say no," Mrs. Pepper nodded, taking off her overall and revealing a home-knitted brown tweed skirt and jumper.

"Is that another of your interests? Knitting?" Kate indicated the clothes.

"Yes, I do that in the evenings. Can't abide to be doing nothing. I knit while I watch the television. My husband can't understand how I do it. How do you watch television and knit? he asks me. You can't do both, he says. Oh, can't I? I say. And I just go on knitting. You wear what I knit, don't you, I say. And he can't think of an answer to that."

Kate made the tea and sat down opposite her. Mrs. Pepper talked on, retailing village gossip, family history and the last comma and full stop of every conversation she had ever had with her husband. Kate listened, offered home-made scones and jam, poured tea and sipped it. She felt as though, unawares, she had slipped into the path of a huge tidal wave. Her mind was battered to and fro under the impact of Mrs. Pepper.

Mrs. Butler returned from her ministrations to the newcomer in the stable, an old riding school pony which had been sold when the owner died and was to have ended as horsemeat if a kindly neighbour had not stepped in to save it, and looked at them in amusement.

"Any tea left for me? Then you must come out with me to milk the goats, Kate. You'll soon learn how to do it."

"How is the pony?" Kate asked.

Mrs. Pepper smiled at them both and removed herself to do some more work upstairs. Kate sighed as the door closed behind her.

Mrs. Butler laughed. "Mrs. Pepper is quite an experience, isn't she? The pony is cheering up. He'll have to stay indoors for a few days until he's settled in with us. Poor chap, he had a near miss with the slaughterhouse!"

Kate went out to learn how to milk the goats that afternoon. Mrs. Butler was a patient teacher, and Kate's uneasy clumsiness amused her. When the goat kicked over Kate's bucket for the third time, Kate groaned, but Mrs. Butler laughed.

"That's enough for today. You'll have sore wrists tomorrow. Milking is like riding a bike—once learnt you never forget, but it may take a while to pick up the knack. That's all it is—a knack. You'll learn, my dear."

"What shall I do now? I don't feel I'm earning my keep, Mrs. Butler. I seem to have so little to do."

"You can take the dogs for a long walk. They need exercise."

"Could I do some of the cooking for you now and then? I would enjoy that, and it would leave you more free time for yourself."

Mrs. Butler looked at her sideways. "You mustn't

feel you have to work yourself to death, Kate. I'm more than happy with the way you're working."

Kate went to fetch the dogs with a feeling of uneasiness which lay heavily over her heart. If she could have felt really useful in the household she would not have felt so guilty, but she suspected that Mrs. Butler could well manage without her. Her presence was not dictated by any need for assistance with the work. Mrs. Butler had only wanted her as an ally in the war against Sylvia, and Kate had a furtive feeling that the full extent of Mrs. Butler's plot had not yet been revealed, and that, when it was clear, she would find it both distasteful and personally wounding.

So involved with her thoughts was she that she barely noticed where she walked, and was surprised to find herself approaching the far side of the park, where the flint wall was crumbling away, under the impact of weather and age. The stones shone with a blueish tint, where water had run down earlier and been caught in crevices and cracks. The grass was slippery underfoot from the rain. The sky had cleared. The livid hue had gone, leaving a washed blue, shimmering faintly, but illuminating the landscape with a gentle radiance.

The dogs snuffled eagerly forward, paws scrabbling on the ground. Kate saw that there was a gate, narrow and ancient, set in the wall. It hung open on a broken hinge. She pushed it further open. The dogs rushed through, excitedly puffing, and she followed.

She stood in a sloping green pasture. Cows grazed on the other side of the meadow. A few trees offered shade. Beyond lay a field of freshly ploughed and planted crop. It ran on for some distance, fenced in by a well-tended hedge, newly burgeoning with bright green. The ditches were well defined and cleared. Kate had grown up on the edge of the sea, with the country always within walking distance, and she could see at a glance that the farm was well managed. It had a neat, prosperous air.

The farmhouse stood half a mile away, in a square half acre of yards, with clean, well-painted outbuildings. They had been freshly whitewashed lately, she saw, from the way the light struck a dazzle from them Well-kept machinery stood under cover in open sheds. The haystacks were covered, too, and protected from the weather.

While she stood there, staring with appreciation around her, she suddenly saw a young man coming across the meadow towards her. He was very tall, with light brown hair tumbled across his thin face, and he walked fast, with an easy swing.

His jeans were muddy. His blue shirt flapped open at the neck. On one thin arm he wore a broad wrist watch.

When he was within earshot he called, "Hi. Come on over to the house for tea!"

Kate stood, uncertainly, smiling back at him, while the dogs tumbled over each other, barking, in order to show their welcome for him.

He reached her side and looked her over with interest. "I know who you are, you know. You're Aunt Elaine's new protégée. Right?"

She laughed. "Right. Kate Fox," and held out her hand.

He solemnly took it and held it, grinning after a moment. "I didn't think you were Dr. Livingstone. I'm Jimmy Whitney. My old man farms here."

"I've heard about him from Mrs. Butler and Mrs. Pepper," she nodded. "It's a very neat farm."

Jimmy laughed loudly. "Tell the old man that—he'll be thrilled. He'd have me painting the hens white if they stood still long enough! One thing that drives him mad is to see a dirty farmyard. I tell him he's got a complex about it."

"I expect it pays in the long run. Less disease, less waste."

Jimmy stared at her. "Do you come from a farming family, by any chance?"

"My father was a vet," she explained. "When I was little I went out with him to visit farms in the countryside where we lived. I suppose I took an interest."

"Well, come and take an interest in us," he said. "It isn't often that I get the chance to meet a girl as pretty as you."

She blushed. "Thank you, but have you never seen Sylvia?"

He grimaced. "Oh, I've seen her. She never sees me, though. Looks straight through me as if I were a pane of glass. You didn't know I was the invisible man, did you? Well, I am. Anyone who earns less than ten thousand a year is invisible to Miss Sylvia."

"Does Nicholas earn that much?" Kate stared, open-mouthed.

Jimmy laughed. "No, I don't suppose so, but then he has Sanctuary, hasn't he? He doesn't need to earn so much. He owns all this . . ." He threw his arm in a grand sweep around the dreaming countryside, over green fields and flat, well-drained acres of good arable land. The countryside was a perfect example of the domestic landscape, patched into odd shapes by trimmed hedges and meandering ditches, punctuated by the occasional elm or oak to give variety to the eye.

"It is lovely," she sighed.

"Isn't it just?" Jimmy nodded. "My old man would give his eye teeth to buy this land, but with Nick earning a fair old crust at his job, he has no need to sell land, and of course, Aunt Elaine will see to it that Nick never feels the urge to so much as sell one acre of Sanctuary estate."

"She loves the place, doesn't she?"

Jimmy looked at her with interest. "I've always thought that Aunt Elaine feels far more loyalty towards the place than Nick because he was born to it, and familiarity breeds . . . if not contempt, at least a sort of blindness. While she is only related by marriage, and she always seemed twice as keen as the rest of the family."

"Like a convert to a religion, you mean, being more fervent than someone born in it?"

"That's it exactly," Jimmy agreed.

They walked down towards the farmhouse, the dogs eagerly scouting the surrounding land. The cows lifted lazy heads to stare, but seemed indifferent to the dogs.

"The cows don't mind dogs?" she asked Jimmy, and he laughed.

"They know these are harmless."

In the farmyard they found Jimmy's father, slouching across the swept concrete with his old green felt hat pulled down low and the elbows out of his old green jersey.

"You disgusting object, you," Jimmy said with affectionate scorn. "Here am I, bringing a pretty young lady to tea, and we find you wearing your jumble sale clothes!"

Old James turned, grinning cheerfully. "This is a pleasant surprise. Perhaps the young lady darns?"

Kate answered his smile as she shook hands. "I'll be glad to mend your jersey for you."

"It comes of having no woman in the house," he said. "I can't tend to the farm and play housewife at the same time."

"Mrs. Cooper is waiting for the call, Dad," Jimmy murmured teasingly.

His father's rosy features drew together in a scowl. "God bless my soul, boy! That woman . . ."

Jimmy gave Kate a grin of proffered conspiracy. "Dad knows very well that Mrs. Cooper would step in at a moment's notice—she's always made it quite clear that she's willing to cheer his later years, shed sunshine on his life's downward slope . . ."

Old James threw a handful of straw at him and stamped away, shaking his head, muttering, "Impudence!"

"I can't really stay for tea," Kate told Jimmy. "I didn't think you were serious. I have to walk back now. Mrs. Butler will wonder where I am."

"We have a telephone—ring her."

"No, I couldn't do that. I work for her. I'm not a guest in the house."

"Surely you have some time off?"

Kate looked blank. "I'd never thought of it. I have so little to do even when I am working that I hadn't thought of asking for time off."

"Disgraceful! The union would have something to say about that! You must do something about it as soon as possible, then I can take you into Malden to the pictures."

"I haven't been to the cinema for ages," she exclaimed.

"High time you did, then! Will you do that? Tell Aunt Elaine I want to date you."

Kate blushed. "Well, thank you, but . . ."

He groaned. "Oh, come on . . . don't be cruel! If you knew how empty my life would be, if you said no, you couldn't refuse!"

Very pink, but smiling, she shook her head at him. "You don't expect me to believe that, of course?" He was an engaging young man, and she suspected, very popular with her own sex, for all his pretended loneliness. That carefree, cheerful manner would be quite attractive to most girls, even if Sylvia ignored him, and Kate felt sure that he had a string of girl-friends somewhere.

"What do I have to do to prove my need? Cry?

Stand on my head?" He did a graceful handstand and gazed at her, upside down, his feet waving way above her head. "There . . . are you convinced?"

She walked away, laughing, despite her cynical disbelief in his plea. Jimmy righted himself and hurried after her.

"I'll walk back with you," he announced, adding complacently, "That will give me time to persuade you to agree . . ."

"I'm very flattered by the invitation," she said, "but don't you think I should wait until I've been at Sanctuary for a while before I start asking for time off? Another time, perhaps?"

"You look so pliant, so sweet and feminine," he complained. "Why are you being hard and unyielding to me?"

She saw Nicholas suddenly, coming slowly towards them through the green pasture, wearing biscuit-coloured slacks and a chocolate-coloured pullover.

"Where the hell have you been?" he demanded tersely as he reached them. "Aunt Elaine has been worrying herself sick over you."

"I'm sorry—" Kate began unhappily.

"It was my fault," Jimmy broke in quickly, smiling at her. "I persuaded her to pay us a short visit."

"She's old enough to say no," snapped Nicholas. "And old enough to know that she doesn't pay private visits during working hours. She was supposed to be walking the dogs, not flirting."

"I was not flirting," Kate snapped, her colour and her temper flaring together. "I'm sorry if I walked too far, but I didn't realise how late it was getting."

"Look here, Nick," Jimmy said, "I think you're being a bit unreasonable . . ."

"Your opinion is irrelevant," Nick said coolly. "Goodbye, Jimmy." Putting a hand under Kate's elbow, he walked her away, fast, ignoring the boisterous attempts made by the dogs to attract his attention.

"I thought you were a sensible girl," Nick said to her cuttingly. "Surely you can see that young Jimmy is a flirt? Have you no common sense, wandering off with him like that, without letting anyone know where you were?"

"Mrs. Butler told me to take the dogs for a long walk. She didn't say I should be back by any specified time."

"Your own sense must have told you that you'd gone too far," he said angrily.

Kate was silent because she was near to tears. For a while they walked in silence, then he glanced sidelong at her averted little face. His own face softened. "All right, I'm a male chauvinist pig. I blew my top. I've had a hard day at the office and a difficult drive home, and when I had to come out looking for you when I got home at last, I was irritated. I shouldn't have taken my temper out on you. I'm sorry."

His capitulation brought a queer roughness into her throat. She said huskily, "It doesn't matter."

"It does," he disagreed. "I have no business behaving like a brute to you. I expect you already had a pretty shrewd idea of Jimmy's character. What did he say to you?"

"He was asking me to go out with him," she said, without thinking.

His face froze again, the grey eyes icy. "Jimmy has dated every girl for miles. He's labelled strictly for fun, and I doubt if you're old enough to know how to deal with him."

"I'm not a child," she retorted indignantly.

"Aren't you?" His brows lifted in an infuriating smile.

"No, I'm not," she insisted. "I liked Jimmy. He was kind and friendly."

"Oh, no doubt," he murmured sardonically.

"In any case, I think it's my business who I go out with. You know nothing about me. We only met a couple of days ago. You may have given me a job, but that doesn't give you the right to dictate who I go out with."

He was withdrawn, his profile unyielding. They walked up towards the house in silence. Then he looked at her in unsmiling scrutiny. "I should have known that it was useless to discuss the matter with you. You're determined to test the water, aren't you? I suppose you were shut up in that house with your aunt for so long that you feel you've missed out on the gay things of life, and I can understand that. But you can pay too dearly for such things, you know.

"Experience is worth any amount of theory," Kate said. "I don't think anyone learns from other people's pasts, only from their own."

"Oh, it's experience you want, is it?" He bit the words out, his face dark red, his eyes furious. "Well, how about this?"

He pulled her into his arms so that she jerked off balance, falling against him. His head bent. She was taken so much by surprise that she just stood still while he kissed her, neither responding nor struggling. His mouth was hard, demanding, strange. She had never been kissed before. When he lifted his head she stood in passive incredulity, her hands trembling, pale and stricken.

Nicholas was breathing fast. For a moment they stood, like statues. Then he groaned. "Oh, God! Why the hell did I do that? What on earth can I say?"

Kate ran from him, then, fleeing into the house. He stared after her, then turned on his heel and strode into the darkness.

At an upstairs window Mrs. Butler stared down, her blue eyes wide and very bright in her lined old face. She smiled. Her gaze moved gently over Sanctuary's land.

"Well, Mistress Sylvia," she breathed triumphantly to herself, "we'll see who has the trump card now!"

CHAPTER FOUR

KATE slept badly. Conscience pricked badly, making a poor bedfellow. Her dislike of Sylvia somehow made the whole incident even worse—increased her guilt and made her question her own integrity. Her aunt had been strict, a Christian in an older mould, teaching virtues which modern civilisation seemed to find unnecessary. Kate had never before been faced with any choice which caused her pain. Now she lay awake, tossing restlessly, trying to decide her future course.

Should she leave Sanctuary at once? Or was that pure melodrama?

She flew from one extreme to the other. At one time she laughed at herself for taking seriously what to Nicholas had been a moment's impulse, forgotten as soon as he walked away.

Then she felt again the impact of his mouth, the hot flood of colour in her own face as she stumbled out of his arms—and she sat up in her bed, shivering.

When she fell asleep at last it was into a sleep so deep, so heavy, that dawn passed into full sunlight before she woke, sandy-eyed and yawning.

After a hasty, lukewarm bath she dressed in jeans and sweater and fled downstairs. The kitchen was sunnily empty. The kittens slept in their basket and the old clock on the shelf above the range ticked busily, with a sound like bees in clover, full of satisfied complacency.

She ate breakfast hurriedly and went out to find Mrs. Butler. There was no sign of her in the gardens or the paddocks, so Kate returned to the house, full of contrition for having left all her share of the early morning work to her employer.

Voices drew her to the front of the house, so rarely in use that she barely knew her way around it yet. The front door stood open. In a shaft of sunlight Mrs. Butler's white hair shone like filigree silver.

"No, no—I don't need any of these things. I'm too old for such frivolities."

"Too old?" The voice was like warm treacle, thick and dark. "No woman should ever say that. Even if you were a hundred you should want to look your best."

"Who's to say that my best needs any artificial aids?" Mrs. Butler was cool, a little wary of this man.

"You don't use lavender?" The man's voice was teasing, knowing. "Lady, don't tell me—I'm an expert!" He sniffed loudly. "Nice, very nice, but I can offer you something more in keeping with your personality."

"I grow my lavender, I dry it and I hang it in my wardrobes and drawers, in little silk bags." Mrs. Butler was triumphant. "I always have, always will."

Kate watched from the shadows of the hall. The man, short, thick-set, with thick oily black hair and a round, humorous face, smiled at the old woman, lifting his shoulders in an age-old gesture of resignation.

"I know when I'm beaten. So I've wasted a journey! It happens. Thank you for listening to me." He was about to turn away when he caught sight of Kate and his smile widened once more. "But is the young lady so hard-hearted? Can I show you what I've got to sell, miss?"

Mrs. Butler moved sideways, but too late. He was inside the hall, moving swiftly, for a man of such bulk, his suitcase under his arm.

"The light here is terrible—if I may?" He was off again, darting from door to door, peering into rooms. "Now, in here you'll be able to see my goods properly!" He was in the drawing-room, putting his case on the occasional table by the window.

Indignantly Mrs. Butler stalked up to him. "Were you invited into this house? You come barging in here, bold as you please . . ."

"I won't take up more than five minutes of your time—I swear it." He was pulling out bottles, packets, boxes—creams, perfumes, hair lacquer, all expensively packaged and heavily scented. Kate looked apologetically at Mrs. Butler, shrugging her shoulders.

"I'm sorry," she told the salesman, "but I really don't want anything—I have enough of such things already." Why was it so difficult to be rude to these people? She resented his impudence, wished he would go, yet could not bring herself to be downright rude to him. For to order him out of the house would seem like rudeness—she knew that it was illogical. How dared he walk into the house without an invitation, ignore their coldness, deliberately force them to be unveiled in their hostility before he would leave!

All the time he was talking, extolling the virtues of this or that bottle, and all the time his small black eyes darted around the room, examining the furniture and the ornaments on the mantelshelf and the tables. There was a fine cabinet in one corner, filled with old china. His eye lingered there.

"No," Kate said firmly, "I don't want anything—please go, now. You have no right to be in here. If you don't leave . . ."

He cut her short, darting to the cabinet. "I'm going, I'm going. Lovely china—some of it good stuff. I suppose you wouldn't sell any of it?"

"Certainly not!" Mrs. Butler was angry now. "Kate, go and ring the police . . ."

"Now, is that nice? I said I was going . . ." The man picked up his case, his samples and was walking out of the room as he spoke. In the hall, with them close behind him, he sauntered casually along, still talking cheerfully. He dropped one of his samples, bent to pick it up and took some time to stand up straight again. Kate saw his hand touch, in a strange stroking motion, the old umbrella stand beside the table on which lay hats, gloves, scarves of the household, rarely used and gathering dust.

He gave them a wide, friendly smile. "No hard feelings, ladies. Good day."

Mrs. Butler slammed the door shut. Kate was kneeling beside the umbrella stand, inspecting it. Mrs.

Butler lifted an eyebrow.

"What are you doing?" she asked.

"Could this be valuable?"

Kate's urgent tone amused the old woman. She laughed and looked at the tall china pot, yellow with age, cracked here and there, all the colours painted on its sides fading to gentle shadows of themselves; misty blues and greens.

"A Victorian umbrella stand? Now is it likely? Why should you imagine such a thing?"

"He seemed very interested in it."

"Perhaps he once had one like it—or perhaps he's just fond of Victorian objects. Many people are—they like the solidity of Victoriana, you know, the vanished glory of a secure age. I'm too much a part of that time, myself, to feel such an emotion. I detest Victorian stuff—heavy, clumsy work. Vulgar."

"You like the eighteenth century?"

Mrs. Butler smiled. "I like things that work, my dear—chairs you can sit on, tables that stand on four good legs. I'm a practical down to earth woman."

Kate laughed. "That's why you prefer the kitchen."

"It's a warm, living room—not a tomb!" Mrs. Butler stood at the door of the drawing-room, looking round the walls. "These rooms were all furnished just as they are now when I first came here—I haven't touched a stick of furniture. I feel an intruder in this part of the house. It was intended to be very grand."

Gently, Kate said, "Just as Sylvia intends it to be?"

Mrs. Butler shut the door with a bang. Kate watched her walk away, straight-backed and erect of head, and sighed.

Sylvia arrived in the middle of the morning, shooting up the drive in her sports car, making a violent commotion on the horn. The horses kicked up startled hooves and fled to another part of the park. Kate, who had been inspecting them for signs of wear and tear on their shoes, since a visiting blacksmith was due any day, looked round in dismay.

Sylvia braked, waving. Kate walked reluctantly over to meet her, saying good morning in a politely colourless voice.

"Are you ready?" Sylvia demanded without answering.

"Ready?"

A flicker of irritation in the lovely face. "Surely Nick told you I was coming to drive you into town to get some new clothes?"

Kate flushed angrily. "I think I can be trusted to buy my own clothes, thank you. I can't just drive off and leave Mrs. Butler . . ."

"We'll go up to the house to tell her. You'll have to change, anyway. You can't go out in those filthy jeans." The green eyes flicked at the mud-stained edges of the legs.

Kate felt her spine stiffen. Rage made her brown eyes hard, her lips compress.

Sylvia looked up at her, leaning back in her car, a smile touching the corners of the exquisite mouth. "Get in!"

Kate still hesitated, searching for the words with which to refuse, words which would somehow express her anger yet remain at least on the surface totally courteous.

"Look," Sylvia drawled, "if you can't afford to buy some clothes Nick will advance you the money from your salary!"

"I've got plenty of money," Kate retorted indignantly, forgetting the speech she had been carefully preparing.

"Then get in, for goodness' sake," Sylvia said wearily.

Kate found herself obeying. In her own bedroom, a few moments later, she stared at herself in critical irritation. She looked like a schoolgirl, she thought. Or even a schoolboy, in these old jeans, her figure slender and boyish, with the clean fresh-air glow in her face, innocent of make-up as it was.

With a self-dismissing shrug she hurriedly slipped into a pale lemon sweater and tan skirt, brushed her sleek brown hair and put on some make-up.

When she ran down the stairs Sylvia regarded her carefully, one thin eyebrow flickering upward in amused scorn. "Well, at least it's an improvement."

The drawled words stung, as they were meant to do. Kate bit back a retort. Had she really spent half the night guiltily wondering if she ought to leave Sanctuary rather than come between Sylvia and Nick? What man in his senses could even look at her with this almond-eyed blonde around? Her vanity had blinded her briefly. Now she was clear-eyed once more, seeing things as they were rather than as she would have liked them to be.

Her mind jumped involuntarily at that thought. As she would like to be? Was that it? She closed her eyes and sighed heavily.

"What's up? Am I going too fast?" Sylvia, glancing sidelong, had caught her expression and misread it. She laughed, accelerating even more, her green eyes malicious.

Kate did not like to drive so fast, but she would have died rather than admit as much to this girl. She gritted her teeth and suffered in silence. After a while Sylvia slowed a little and soon after that they arrived at Malden, having exchanged no word on the journey.

When they had parked, Sylivia took Kate to a newly opened boutique in the main street. A tall girl with short, curly brown hair greeted them politely. She clearly knew Sylvia very well, but equally obviously did not like her.

"Hello, Helen—I've brought you a client. Do I get any commission?"

Smiling at Kate, the other girl held out her hand. "Hello, client. I'm Helen Cochrane."

Sylvia stiffened. "Sorry, did I forget to introduce you? This is Kate Fox, she's my fiancé's secretary."

Helen had not glanced away from Kate's face. "So you want some new clothes, Kate? Your colouring is useful—you can wear almost any colour. What sort of thing are you looking for? Dress? Coat?"

"The lot," Sylvia drawled, despite Helen's determined cold-shouldering. "Pastel shades would be the best bet."

"Oh, I don't think we'll limit ourselves to colour

for the moment." Helen took Kate's elbow and led her towards the old-gold curtain which was draped across the entrance to the fitting-room. It matched the rich piled gold carpet exactly and was a perfect foil to the dark blue of the walls.

Sylvia stood, a spot of hard red in her cheeks, staring at them. Over her shoulder, Helen murmured, "Oh, don't wait, Sylvia—I'm sure you have plenty of other things to do! Kate can meet you in the Copper Kettle for lunch in an hour's time!"

Sylvia, dismissed in so casual a fashion, slammed out of the shop without a word. Helen laughed.

"Exit Lady Macbeth!"

Kate was taken aback and stared at her. "Not that bad, surely?"

Helen shrugged. "I don't know—Sylvia is inclined to go about ordering everyone to have their heads cut off."

"More like the Red Queen in *Alice* than Lady Macbeth!"

Helen grinned at her. "Maybe. I've never liked Sylvia, nor she me—she brought you here today to emphasise the fact that I'm in trade while she's marrying the lord of the manor."

Kate was amused. "Nicholas? That doesn't sound like him."

"Oh, he wouldn't recognise the description, but Sylvia is the most awful snob, and she's determined that he shall assert his 'position'—as she sees it. Sylvia and I were at school together. She's always thought that one day she would marry well—she has an acquisitive mind."

Kate remembered Mrs. Butler saying something like that. She hurriedly changed the subject.

"Have you got any dresses with a longer line? I prefer a low hem."

"Strip to your undies and I'll bring some suitable things in to you," Helen told her.

When she returned she gave Kate's very plain underclothes a long, disapproving stare. "You need new lingerie as well—a girl should be pretty from the skin outwards. Top dressing is only half the answer."

She selected a gay green dress of jersey wool. It slid down over Kate as if it had been made for her, fitting snugly at bust and waist, but flaring out at the hip.

"Semi-Russian style," Helen explained. The calf-length skirt flew out as Kate turned to face the mirror. Around the neck ran a choker of black braid, which was echoed at the hem, in a line of three.

"It suits you. Gives you colour and style—I think you ought to have your hair re-styled, you know." Helen considered her, head to one side. "A page-boy bob, I think—give you a new image. Why not really go for the Russian look? I've got something else which will follow through with the same general look."

Kate felt a timid excitement stirring. "Do you really think—?" She looked at herself, her cheeks pink, her eyes bright. The vivid green deepened the impact of her colouring, gave a new drama to the muted brown of her hair and eyes.

Helen was decided. "Of course—just look in the mirror! You need bold styles and colours. Pastels would make you invisible. Why else do you think Sylvia was so keen for you to wear pastel shades? She wanted to make you look negative."

Kate flushed even deeper. "Why on earth should she bother?"

"Don't ask me," Helen shrugged. "If you don't know the answer I certainly don't. Knowing Sylvia I'd say she was making sure Nick never noticed you. She may be sure of herself, but she's the cold-headed sort who make doubly certain when they can."

"She can't be afraid of me!" Kate was pale now, her colour gone.

Helen was indifferent. "Probably not, but she was always the malicious sort. She just likes to quash all possible opposition, as a matter of course."

She went off to look for other garments and brought back a peacock-blue trouser suit, with a loose tunic belted at the waist, bringing in a Russian look again.

An hour later Kate had bought a pile of clothes, including several new skirts and some delicious, fragile, floating blouses in crêpe, with loose sleeves tightly cuffed at the wrist and neat round collars which gave her a little-girl look. She had also insisted on buying two new sweaters, polo-neck and cowl-neck, one scarlet, the other yellow.

"I must have something to wear when I'm working with the horses. I can hardly wear my trouser suit!"

They walked amicably to the Copper Kettle together. There was no sign of Sylvia in the crowded dining-room. Helen left Kate there, shaking hands warmly, and returned to her shop. Kate ordered, after a while, and ate a simple salad. Sylvia had still not appeared, so she went back to the dress shop.

"Why not take the opportunity to have your hair fixed?" Helen suggested.

"I ought to get back to Sanctuary. I do work there, remember."

"How can you leave without Sylvia? The bus is very unreliable. It only runs a few times a day, and I don't know when it's due next."

Kate was undecided, so Helen picked up the phone and began to dial.

"Are you ringing the bus company?"

"No—Nick," said Helen firmly.

"Please, I'd rather not . . ." Kate was cut off in her stammered dismay when Helen spoke into the telephone.

She was put through to Nick at once, and greeted him in a cheerful, intimate fashion. After a few friendly remarks, she explained the situation. Suddenly she handed the phone to Kate, smiling.

"He wants to speak to you."

Kate nervously said, "Hallo."

"Helen says you want to have your hair done and buy some new shoes—will you be ready to leave at five? I'll drive you back myself if you can be at the Copper Kettle around five." He sounded abrupt but courteous.

"Thank you," she said lamely.

There was a pause, then he said tersely, "Five,

then? Goodbye." The phone clicked at his end. She put the receiver down carefully.

Helen looked enquiringly at her. "Well?"

"He'll pick me up at five at the Copper Kettle."

"That's marvellous. Come on, I'll take you down to the hairdresser."

Feeling more like a puppet than a human being, Kate allowed herself to be hustled along to the hairdresser's shop. Helen gave her instructions clearly and left. Kate sat, watching in awed surprise, as the clever scissors clipped and darted around her head.

Later, seated under the dryer, she was dreamily watching the passing traffic when she recognised Sylvia's car. A tangle of some sort had developed. Sylvia was impatiently hooting at the car in front. Beside her, his arm along the back of the seat, watching her with open amusement, was a rather distinguished man with silver-grey hair and a lean, still handsome face. His suit was elegant well-cut, expensive. He was, Kate judged, well on the wrong side of forty.

Sylvia's father? Kate watched them curiously. Whoever he was, the stranger found Sylvia fascinating. Suddenly the blonde head turned and Sylvia looked at him in provocative interest.

Again, Kate pondered on their relationship. There was, even at this distance, no doubt as to the intimacy of their acquaintance. But its nature was more difficult to assess.

The traffic cleared. The little sports car shot away. Kate leaned back, frowning.

When her hair was finished, she was delighted with Helen's inspiration. The sleek brown shine, the gentle wave where it curled inwards, gave her a new appearance. Her features were more interesting in their new frame. She was still not exactly pretty, she sighed, but at least it was an improvement.

Helen was far more enthusiastic when she got back to the shop. She walked all round Kate, exclaiming in pleasure.

"What did I tell you? Aren't you delighted?"

"I do like it," Kate admitted.

"Lukewarm! It's an enormous change for the better," Helen said firmly.

Kate laughed. "I'm beginning to feel like the flower girl in *Pygmalion*! I don't feel myself at all."

"Shoes now," instructed Helen.

Kate groaned. "Must I? I'm worn out!"

"Rebirth is tiring, I believe," said Helen blandly. "Don't spoil the ship for a ha'porth of tar! Shoes!"

Wearily Kate followed her to the shoe shop. Soon the floor was littered with open boxes and discarded styles. Helen was inexorable. She would not settle for anything less than perfection. When at last Kate had acquired several pairs of shoes and a pair of elegant sandals, Helen agreed finally to release her.

Laden with parcels and boxes, Kate sat in the dress shop watching the clock. Helen said happily that she would shut up shop early for once, and join Kate for tea in the Copper Kettle.

"We can have a nice cosy chat over a pot of tea and some cakes. I'm starving. I skipped lunch today because my assistant is off sick."

"Don't you close for lunch?"

"No—we get a lot of our custom during lunchtime because so many of the girls from other shops pop in in their lunch break."

They found a corner table and settled down. The waitress brought them a tray of tea, smiled at Helen and wandered away.

"What do you think of Nick?" Helen asked Kate suddenly.

Kate jumped, her cheeks suddenly very pink. "What? Oh . . . h—he seems very pleasant."

Helen looked at her in amusement. "Yes," she said calmly, "he's a charmer. Half the girls in Essex have fallen for Nick at one time. I had a crush on him myself when I was sixteen. I know the signs."

Kate looked away from the probing, too clear-sighted eyes. She hoped Helen was not reading too much into her stammered reply. The sudden question had taken her by surprise.

But Helen was examining the plate of home-made cakes, choosing a slice of butter-iced sponge after a moment, and transferring it to her own plate.

Picking up her fork, she murmured, "Do help yourself!"

Kate hurriedly took a jam tart. It tasted of sawdust and she ate it automatically.

After a moment Helen resumed her theme. "Nick was considered our local Lothario for ages. He took out various girls, but it never seemed serious. Then he met Sylvia—or rather Sylvia made up her mind that Nick would do for her. She'd known him for years, of course, in a distant sort of way. She'd been playing the field, just as Nick had—a new boy-friend every week. None of them were rich enough, so she singled Nick out and soon had him in a corner."

Kate stared at her plate. "You make it sound more like a fight than a love affair!"

"I've never believed Sylvia capable of any honest emotion," Helen said coolly.

"You really don't like her, do you?"

There was a little pause. Helen grinned, lifting her slim shoulders in a shrug. "Never could stand the sight of her—I hate being patronised."

"She's very beautiful."

"She knows it. That's most of the trouble—she's like the Lady of Shalott. She's looked into the mirror for so long that she couldn't bear the sight of life itself. She's self-obsessed."

Kate pushed her plate away. "Poor Nick!" She said it lightly, but her heart was heavy.

"Oh, yes, poor Nick—marriage with Sylvia will be perfect hell, I imagine." Helen frowned. "Unless somebody enlightens him about her, before the knot is tied."

Kate hardly heard her. She was staring across the room, her brown eyes wide and vulnerable. Nick had just come into the Copper Kettle. He was closing the door, his back towards her, and for a brief second Kate could look at him without being observed.

Then he turned, and she felt her heart begin to thud against her ribs, so that she was scared someone would hear it. Her throat felt dry and rough. Her hands were damp with sudden nerves.

What's the matter with me? she asked herself irritably. I'm behaving like a schoolgirl. Vaguely she recalled what Helen had said—was that what was happening to her, was she infatuated with Nicholas, as Helen had been at sixteen?

She brushed the thought away angrily. With an effort she looked at him, smiling calmly.

He stood in front of her, staring at her, the grey glance skimming from her shining brown head to her elegant new shoes. Then he grinned at Helen. "Are you responsible for this transformation? She's a different girl!"

"You approve?" Helen watched him curiously.

Nicholas open his mouth, then closed it again. An odd expression passed over his face. After a moment, he smiled. "You're to be congratulated. You've altered her beyond belief."

Helen laughed. "You'll soon have young men queueing up at Sanctuary for the honour of taking her out!"

Nicholas sat down suddenly. "No doubt," he agreed brusquely.

CHAPTER FIVE

NICK was very quiet as he drove back to Sanctuary. From beneath her half-closed lids Kate watched him, sidelong, his profile silhouetted against the pale dusk of the evening sky. The spring sunshine had evaporated. The dew was falling. A faint, delicious odour still clung to hedge and field, that untraceable scent of spring which is compounded of flowers, new grass and burgeoning leaf.

In this shadowy atmosphere Nick looked suddenly unfamiliar once more. She remembered, with a pang, how he had seemed to her when they first met. How inexplicable are our first impressions, and how hard to pin down later, when constant contact has erased that first clear imprint. How had she seen him then? The executive type, smooth and well-groomed, with a sardonic expression?

Well, she thought wryly, watching him, that was still what he looked like to the casual stranger, no doubt. He was wearing his office clothes, well-tailored, expensive and breathing an air of success. The dark hair was brushed down. The eyes, staring at the road ahead, were a wintry grey as they contemplated some mental problem or other. His well-cut mouth had a sardonic twist to it at this moment, too, as if those thoughts were ironic and made him contemptuous.

Only now she knew what lay beneath this off-putting exterior. He could shed this skin with a shrug of his broad shoulders. The man about town, the successful architect, could in a second become a countryman, casually dressed and relaxed, tolerant, easygoing and charming.

Which was the real man? she wondered suddenly. Was Nick really happier at Sanctuary, in his old clothes, tramping over the fields with Punch, Patch and Poppy? Or was this the real Nick, this elegant stranger with the cool, withdrawn expression, who drove without speaking to her and was a hundred miles from here in his thoughts?

Perhaps that was the real reason for his involvement with Sylvia, that relationship which so disturbed his aunt? Was the Nick who loved Sylvia this man now seated beside her? Was that the real man? Had his aunt lost contact with him while she sought comfort in her dream world at Sanctuary, caring for the animals she rescued because she could no longer cope with the realities of life with Nick?

Kate had never been able to understand why the warm, amiable man who loved his aunt had fallen in love with so hard, so cold a creature as Sylvia.

She had believed until now that the shell Nick assumed when he left Sanctuary was merely a discardable disguise. Now she wondered if, perhaps, the shell were not the real man and the man his aunt thought she knew were truly a disguise.

She shook her head, grimacing. Her thoughts

buzzed in her head like bees in a hollow tree.

Nick laughed. She jumped and looked at him with wide eyes. He smiled at her, his face so warmly familiar that her heart leapt in relief and delight.

"You looked so funny! You've been making the most amazing faces and mumbling away . . ."

She was alarmed. "What did I say?"

"No idea! It was quite incoherent. I thought you'd fallen asleep and I was going to shake you when I saw you shaking yourself." He grinned at her.

"I was trying to work something out," she said evasively.

"Money worries? Anything I can do to help?" He was instantly alert, his eyes concerned.

She shook her head. "Nothing like that."

"Like to tell me about it?"

"Thank you, but it wasn't really that sort of problem."

He shot her a sideways glance. "You . . . you haven't been worrying about us, have you?" He was flushed suddenly. He turned his head back and stared ahead into the dusk. "I mean, I hope I didn't upset you when I kissed you. I lost my temper. I meant to apologise before, but I couldn't get round to it."

"It didn't bother me at all," she said in a manner meant to sound lightly casual, but which came out somehow rather snubbing.

Nick laughed again, but harshly. "I'm glad."

He did not sound glad, she noted unhappily. He sounded . . . But she turned away from the thought as from something that hurt.

"All the same," he went on after a moment, "you must take what I said about Jimmy seriously. I did mean that."

Yes, she thought, you meant *that.* But you didn't mean that kiss, the kiss so stupidly given and so irrevocably received.

"Do you hear me, Kate?" He looked at her angrily, frowning. "Jimmy is a flirt. You seem to get on well with Helen. She knows Jimmy only too well. Ask her if you don't believe me."

"I don't need to do that," she said quietly. She had already recognised Jimmy. Flirts were not that hard to recognise, even for someone as inexperienced as herself. She had not been prepared to listen to Nick, that was all. She had not wanted him to lecture her as though . . . as though she were a *child.* That had been the painful point. Who wants to be considered a child when they are fully aware of their womanhood?

Nick had misunderstood her, however. His face darkened again. "You don't need to? Of course, I forgot how much you want experience! I only hope you won't have to pay too highly for it. Nothing is cheap today, you know."

The harshness of his tone was bitter to her. She did not answer him. It hurt too much to quarrel with him.

After a moment he sighed. "I really don't know what's wrong with me! I seem to be turning into a surly bear. I'm sorry, Kate. I meant well."

"I know," she whispered, smiling without looking

at him.

"Pax?"

She smiled and nodded. "Pax."

He took one hand off the wheel and briefly touched her hands where they lay in her lap. The contact sent an electric shock up her arm to her heart. Never in her life before had she been so aware of the effect emotion can have on the body. Her mind and her body had been separate until now. Suddenly every tiny emotion caused a reaction physically. She was conscious of every pulse in her body, every nerve-end, every beat of her heart. She was even more conscious of Nicholas. His separate intake of breath, his tiny movements, reacted in her. She felt as though there was a physical link between them; as though his blood pumped along her veins too, his breath filled her lungs.

"You're at it again," he said, making her jump violently.

"What?" She blinked at him.

"Dreaming and grimacing . . . You must have the most horrific daydreams since King Kong!"

She laughed, with an effort.

He braked at the gates of Sanctuary, making her sit up in surprise. The lane was empty. There was no other vehicle in sight. The twilight had given a magic significance to every branch, every blade of grass. A pale, fading light irradiated the sky, in the east, and a thin moon swam in a web of transparent cloud. The birds were sleepily calling from their invisible nests. A cloud of midges hovered under one of the trees, rising and falling in a dark cluster.

"Would you like to see the house I've bought for Aunt Elaine?" Nicholas sounded hopeful.

"Well, perhaps it is a bit late..." she said doubtfully. She did not think she could bear much more of his company. She was terrified of betraying herself to him.

"It wouldn't take long," he pleaded.

She hesitated. Nicholas was out of the car in a second and opening her door. She still sat there, uncertain what to do. He bent and extricated her from her seat with a strong, deft arm. Before she could think of anything to say or do, she was walking across the road and in at the small gate of a little cottage.

The garden was overgrown, but she could see, even by the dim dying light, that there were hosts of spring flowers hidden among the weeds and brown brambles. Daffodils, tulips and hyacinths raised strangled heads in the gloom. A lilac tree leaned against the small white fence. Rose bushes reared up here and there, their thorny fingers scraping against the cottage walls as the wind blew.

Nicholas unlocked the front door and ushered her inside. He switched on the light in the hall. It was tiny, the wallpaper a gay splodge of many flowers, giving it the appearance of a mad garden.

The stairs led up on the right. On the left were two doors. Nicholas opened the nearest and waved her onward.

"The parlour—very cosy when it's furnished, as I

remember. It was two small rooms. The last owners knocked it into one room, and I prefer it now. What do you think?"

Kate looked around her. The room was an odd shape, something like the letter T. But it had a certain attraction, especially as the windows had been enlarged to admit as much light as possible

"It is a pretty room," she admitted.

"The kitchen is very modern," said Nick. He showed her into a small, narrow room, fitted with many modern cupboards and some excellent equipment.

"Well?" he demanded.

Kate shrugged. "She'll hate it," she said.

He groaned. "Do you think I don't know that?" He glared around the tiny room. "After the kitchen at Sanctuary! How could she be happy in this box, for all its wonderful gadgets? She hates food anyway. She rarely cooks. The kitchen for her is somewhere to live, not somewhere to cook."

"Then why did you buy it?"

"What else could I do? I've got to do something. This situation can't go on. Sylvia and Aunt Elaine are tearing me in two. I shall go out of my mind if something doesn't resolve the situation."

Kate took the poison point of a spear of pain and drove it into her heart. In a quiet, drained voice she said, "Why not just go ahead and marry Sylvia and let things sort themselves out afterwards?"

He turned to look at her, his eyes narrowing in astonishment. "What?"

She repeated her suggestion. "Once you're married, once it's a *fait accompli*, your aunt will have to come to terms with it. While you hesitate, she can hope that you'll change your mind. Once that hope has vanished she'll face facts."

He was oddly silent. Then he said slowly, "You're right, of course. That's what I must do."

She was surprised that he showed no pleasure in this way out.

He stood, staring down at her, his face thoughtful. "You're a perceptive little thing, Kate. Quiet, gentle Kate . . ." His hand touched her cheek, moved softly downwards to her throat, as though he were caressing one of the cats, the tips of his fingers leaving a track of fire where it had rested, awakening her nerve-ends and making her quiver with happiness.

A transparent glass dome seemed to enclose them for a moment. She saw, heard, nothing but him. He was looking at her with those cool grey eyes. She gazed back, her heart laid bare, moving closer to him without volition, her lips parted in trembling consent.

He bent his head and she lifted her face. For a fraction of a second they almost kissed. Passion did not enter into it. There was only a gentle recognition between them, a sweetness which pierced but did not arouse.

Then the glass dome shattered. Nicholas's face froze. He blinked, as though awakening from a dream. He drew back, his hands dropping from her hurriedly.

"My God," he muttered, "this is becoming a habit. You're far too pretty, Kate. We must avoid these occasions, or you'll think I have a nerve calling Jimmy a flirt!" He tried to grin. "We'd better go."

Mrs. Butler met them at the door, her face anxious. "Punch has disappeared!"

"Disappeared? How long has he been missing?" Nicholas was immediately concerned.

"All day! Ever since you went into Malden, Kate. I suppose you didn't take him with you? I thought perhaps you had!"

"I wouldn't do that without telling you!"

Mrs. Butler sighed. "No, I realised that some time ago. That was when I really became worried. It's not like Punch to miss a meal. He's usually first through the door when I whistle." She looked at Nick pleadingly. "Where can he be?"

"Have you rung the farm? He often goes across there to hunt rabbit, you know, especially if both Kate and I were out and he hadn't had his daily walk."

"It's my fault," Mrs. Butler exclaimed miserably. "I meant to take the dogs for a walk after lunch, but he'd gone by then. That was when I first missed him. Patch and Poppy were asleep in the stable yard, but there was no sign of Punch."

"Odd for him to go off without the other two. They hunt in the pack usually." Nicholas looked down at his clothes. "Look, I'll change and go out to look for him."

"So will I," said Kate, flying upstairs.

"Your dinner!" called Aunt Elaine.

Nick was back on the stairs in five minutes flat, wearing his old jeans and a white sweater. Kate joined him a moment later.

"I'm not hungry," Kate said eagerly. "I had tea at four o'clock."

"Tea?" Nick looked at her in amusement. "That wafer biscuit?"

"I had had a sandwich before you joined us," she flushed.

Mrs. Butler shrugged. "Your dinner will keep hot. Mrs. Pepper left a hotpot in the oven, and that doesn't damage for keeping."

"Come on," said Nick, getting a large hand-torch out of the kitchen. "We'd better stay within earshot of each other. I don't want to have to look for you later."

"I shan't get lost," she assured him indignantly.

"You don't know this countryside yet. In the dark it's quite easy to fall into a ditch. We'll go down to the farm first, calling all the way. If they haven't seen him there, we'll cut across to the river."

"Oh!" Kate had a sudden chilly picture of Punch struggling helplessly in cold water, being dragged along by the impetus of the river.

Nick halted in his stride and looked back at her. His long arm hooked her up, pulling her close against the warmth of his side.

"Stop it, little Miss Fox. Punch has at least ninety-nine lives. Don't think the worst. I'm prepared to bet that he's sleeping, snug as a bug, at the farm, having dined like a king on best steak."

She laughed. "Yes, that's probably what's happened."

The darkness, out here, was absolute now. The moon had gone in behind clouds. There were no stars. The lights of the main road were far, far away. Only the pale path of Nick's torch showed them where they trod. The wind creaked protestingly in the trees. A far-off scream rose suddenly and Kate jumped.

"Don't squeak like that," Nick said. "I almost dropped the torch."

"W—what was that noise?"

"Owl hunting, probably."

She shivered. Hunting what?

"You are a strange little thing," Nicholas told her indulgently. "You shouldn't care so much about things. You will make yourself too vulnerable."

She did not answer. Too vulnerable? She thought of Sylvia, remote and lovely, yet dead in some ways to any sort of human weakness. Better to be too vulnerable than so hard and empty. Was that the choice put before one? To expose oneself to pain, or shut oneself away from all feeling for others, only care for oneself?

I'm unfair to her, she told herself angrily. How do I know what she thinks? But at once she recalled Sylvia's contemptuous look as she spoke of Mrs. Butler, her patronising manner to Helen, even to herself, Kate.

She stumbled once or twice on molehills. Nick had to keep halting for her. She apologised.

"Why don't you go on without me? I'll be all right."

"It looks like it!" He was irritated.

They came down towards the farmhouse, and the lights from it made it easier to see their way. Jimmy met them at the back door, grinning delightedly. But his expression changed when he heard their reason for coming.

"No," he said in concern, "old Punch hasn't been here. How long has he been absent without leave?"

"Most of the day, apparently."

"I'll come with you to search," Jimmy offered.

"Why not search the barns?" suggested Jimmy's father. "Punch may have got into one of them and been locked up."

"Good idea!" said Nick. They all went out to search around the farm, calling loudly, but although the farm dogs set up a raucous noise in response there was no sound of Punch's very individual voice.

They set out then to search the surrounding land, right down to the riverbank and back, but after a further hour it was clear that Punch was not within easy walking distance of Sanctuary, and they went back to the house, leaving Jimmy at the farm on the way.

Mrs. Butler met them at the house, her face eager. Her expression changed as she realised that they had not found the dog.

Nicholas looked at Kate with raised eyebrows. "You need a hot bath—you look like a mudlark!"

She laughed, looking down at her filthy jeans and

sweater. She had fallen so many times during the search that she had long given up any idea of brushing off the mud, and her nose and cheeks were as smeared as her jeans.

"He may have hitched a lift in a car," suggested Nick. "Did anyone call here this morning? You know how much Punch loves to have a ride in a car."

"There was only Sylvia," said his aunt crisply.

Nick went to the telephone and rang her at once. Kate and his aunt stood, waiting, trying not to listen to the conversation.

He returned within a few moments, shaking his head. "No, Sylvia hasn't seen him." He was rather red, Kate saw, and had a tight-lipped air of fury which his aunt observed with great interest.

"Well, we can only wait and see if he turns up," said Mrs. Butler cheerfully. "Kate, go and have that bath. Nick, you'd better have one after her. You can't eat dinner in that condition."

Nicholas curtly nodded. "Yes."

Kate soaked slowly in her bath, feeling her weary muscles relaxing in the scented warmth. Had Nick quarrelled with Sylvia during that brief telephone call?

As he emerged, swathed in the new rose-pink quilted dressing-gown which Helen had persuaded her to add to her list of clothes, she found Nicholas waiting impatiently.

"What were you doing in there?" he demanded in some irritation. "I was about to break the door down and give you artificial respiration!"

Pink and relaxed, her brown hair damply curling, she smiled impishly at him, and passed into her bedroom without answering.

"Women!" He slammed the bathroom door and began to run his bath noisily.

When she got downstairs Mrs. Butler smiled at her, admiring her new appearance.

"You've even had your hair done in a new way!"

"A page-boy bob, yes. Do you like it?"

"Very much! It makes you look quite different. Don't you agree, Nick?" looking over her shoulder with an amused smile.

Kate didn't turn. Her heart leapt and, ignoring this traitorous feeling, she pretended indifference to his response.

"She looks very nice," said Nick tamely.

"Very nice? Oh, Nick," reproached his aunt. "Are you blind?"

His voice was husky, no doubt from the steamy bath. "No," he said flatly. "I'm not blind." Then, suddenly, in a voice sharpened by hope, "And I'm not deaf, or mad, either—isn't that Punch barking somewhere?"

They all stood, transfixed. Faint and far-off came the weak barking.

"It's coming from upstairs," said Nick, running.

They followed. The sound came from the attics. Nick followed it like a hound on the scent and flung open the door of the small room.

"I was in here this morning looking for something in one of the trunks," said Mrs. Butler. "I must have locked him in when I left . . ."

"But where is he?" asked Nick, staring around the small, dusty room.

Then from a motheaten tangle of old blankets crawled a weary animal, lifting his head with eager pleading, whining and licking their hands as they reached him.

"He's ill!" Nicholas touched the damp, perspiring flanks with a gentle hand.

"That's why he didn't answer us! He was asleep, sick . . ."

"He's been sick," Nick indicated. "Poor old lad, what is it?"

"I'll call the vet," Kate offered, leaping for the stairs.

The vet arrived within fifteen minutes and examined Punch carefully. He was slightly better now, able to lift his head with less difficulty.

"He's been poisoned," said the vet. "Fortunately, I think he's managed to expel most of the poison when he vomited, and he's slept most of the day in an effort to fight off the effects. He may have saved his own life. I'll take him with me, just in case the poison is more serious, but I think he'll be all right."

"I'll come with you," said Mrs. Butler.

"Nothing you can do, dear lady," said the vet. "Much better to stay here and look about for the poison. It may be lying around anywhere. Other animals may take it."

"What sort of poison?" asked Nicholas.

"Could be anything—dogs will eat whatever they

find! Rat poison, weed-killer, chemicals of some sort ... who knows? Just check on his usual haunts. Early tomorrow morning will do—in daylight."

When he had gone they had a rather subdued meal. He rang two hours later to tell them that he had got a laboratory analysis of the contents of Punch's stomach. The poison was probably some form of weed-killer. It was in a diluted form, possibly accidentally deposited on some animal. Did Punch eat mice, for instance? That might have been the source.

But they found the source easily enough next day when they discovered a little pool of weed-killer spilled on the floor in the small greenhouse behind the kitchen garden.

"I must have done it," moaned Mrs. Butler in terrible self-reproach, her face white.

"You left the top off the bottle and Punch knocked the bottle over and drank some of the contents," said Nick. "Don't be too upset, Aunt Elaine. Accidents happen. You must remember to put the top back on the bottle again in future."

"I may have killed Punch," she whispered faintly.

"I think he's going to survive! The vet did say that as he's passed the first twenty-four hours without expiring he's not likely to do so now!" Nick's voice was cheerful and coaxing, a little teasing.

"It isn't funny, Nick!" Her vivid blue eyes glared at him.

"I know, darling," he said gently. "But it isn't the end of the world, either. You made a mistake! You're human. Just put it behind you now and forget it."

"I shall never forget it!"

Kate put an arm around her. "Of course you won't forget it! Come and have a cup of tea, then we'll drive in to see Punch and bring him home."

She looked back at Nick, shaking her head reproachfully. He had not handled his aunt very well. Nick shrugged his inability to understand the female mind.

"I shall never use weed-killer again," said Mrs. Butler in a passionate whisper. "I won't take such a risk ever again."

"You don't need it, anyway," Kate said. "I'll do the weeding for you in future, and I'm not poisonous!"

Mrs. Butler laughed. Nick, following them into the house, gave a groan of apprehension.

"I don't like the sound of this! I have a shrewd suspicion that it's me who'll be doing the weeding around here!"

"Put the kettle on, Nick," Kate told him. "Shall we feed the kittens, Mrs. Butler? They look as though they could do with a saucer or two of milk."

"Why don't you call me Aunt Elaine?" came the plaintive reply. "I keep asking you to call me that."

"She's shy," Nick said tolerantly, smiling at Kate's pink-cheeked confusion.

"Have you put the kettle on yet?" Kate demanded crossly.

He laughed. "What a monstrous regiment of women I'm surrounded by! Why do I put up with it?"

"You like it," said his aunt softly, her smile secret.

CHAPTER SIX

SYLVIA lounged on a rough garden seat, her sinuous body sheathed in silver-blue silk jersey pants and shirt. The loose mass of her hair fell into a perfect frame around her face as she tilted her head to smile at Nick.

"You will be at my party next week, won't you? You won't let business interfere with that? If it's fine I planned to have a barbecue in the field next door to our garden—if it rains, we can eat indoors."

"I can't see why anything should interfere," he said vaguely, looking across the garden as the dogs came into sight.

Patch and Poppy snuffled up to him, tails wagging, eyes bright and hopeful. Nick, grinning, patted them, and they became ecstatic. When their enthusiasm took them too close to her, Sylvia's red mouth tightened. The green eyes were frozen with distaste.

"Keep them off me, Nick!"

He looked at her in frowning silence, surprised by the sudden sharpness of her tone.

Unaware for once of his reaction, she went on irritably, "They shower my clothes with hairs. This material picks up everything, and it takes hours to brush it off later."

"Down!" Nick spoke firmly to the dogs. Taking

hold of their collars, he pulled them back. They sat, reluctantly, tongues wagging.

Sylvia, engrossed in the inspection of her pants for signs of the attentions which the dogs had given her, did not even notice Nick's grim silence or the long, cool look he was giving her.

Kate suddenly ran from the house, flushed and excited. "Nick! Nick! The vet just rang! Punch can come home!"

His face lit up. "That's wonderful news!" He smiled at her. "Calm down, Kate! What have you been doing this morning?"

"Grooming the donkeys." She laughed, her brown eyes warm with amusement. "When I could get them to stand still! Their coats are improving, you know. I've noticed a change even in the short time I've been here. All the rest and good food is working wonders."

Sylvia lifted her head. The green eyes flicked over Kate. "Still wearing those filthy old jeans, I see! Some people are incorrigible." Her disdainful drawl brought Nick's eyes to her again.

She did not notice him, her attention concentrated on Kate. The other girl was automatically fondling the dogs, her slim hands gently rubbing their ears and throats.

"Don't let those animals go—I don't want them near me!" Sylvia forgot to hide her shrill dislike.

"I'll take them into the house," Kate said quietly, turning to go.

"Good," Sylvia snapped. "And bring us a jug of lemonade out here—I'm parched! Plenty of ice, too."

"She isn't a servant," Nick said curtly.

Sylvia was suddenly still, the blonde head swinging towards him, the green eyes narrowed in thought.

"She does work here, doesn't she?" The tone was gentle and innocent.

He was dark red. "As a secretary, not a domestic servant! And anyway, this is Saturday. She's allowed some time off to enjoy herself."

Sylvia watched him, glittering and beautiful in her silver-blue clothes, as tensed as an animal scenting danger, her eyes fixed on his face in wary contemplation.

"That reminds me," she murmured. "Kate, Jimmy Whitney sent you a message—he wants to take you out tonight. Will you ring him if you can't come? Otherwise he'll be here at seven o'clock and wants you to wear your prettiest dress."

Kate looked sideways at Nick. His grey eyes met hers in a savage stab. Flushing, she moved away, her head bent. He stared angrily at the pale curve of her neck, where the heavy, bobbed brown hair fell away.

Sylvia watched them both, eyes narrowed. She had her face under control now. Any trace of rage had been carefully erased from her features, and when Nick turned back to her she was smiling sweetly.

"I must drive over to fetch Punch home. You might as well come with me." His voice was hardly eager.

Sylvia uncoiled herself and followed him into the house. Nick ran upstairs to find his car keys. Mrs. Butler, mincing meat on the kitchen table, threw

Sylvia a hostile glance. The dogs lay under the table beside the basket of kittens.

Sylvia waited impatiently, ignoring Mrs. Butler in her turn. The two women were accustomed to this silent warfare.

One of the dogs ran up to greet Sylvia. She pushed him away, and when he came back undeterred, gave him a kick.

"Don't kick my dogs!" Mrs. Butler went white with rage.

"Keep them away from me, then! I don't see why I should be forced to put up with your animals every time I come here."

"You have an alternative!"

"Oh, yes, you would like me to stay away from this house, wouldn't you? It would just suit your book. Well, I won't be driven away by your dirty animals."

"Dirty? My dogs are not dirty!"

"All dogs are unhygienic," Sylvia snapped. "I think it's disgusting, having all these animals in the kitchen, infecting the food you eat. Those kittens probably have fleas, and I'm sure these dogs have them. Look at the way they're always scratching!" She watched with cold amusement as the other woman grew rigid with pure hatred.

"You . . . you . . ." Mrs. Butler was incoherent with rage.

"I'm not surprised somebody poisoned one of them," Sylvia added sweetly. "I've often wanted to poison one of them myself."

She heard Nick on the stairs. With a last triumphant smile she walked out of the kitchen, leaving Mrs. Butler engulfed in vast and bitter fury.

"One day I'll kill that girl!" she told the dogs on a gasp. They looked sympathetic, but their brown eyes were more interested in the meat she was preparing than in the little scene which had just passed.

When Nick returned with Punch he was looking grim. Aunt Elaine glanced past him.

"Where's Sylvia?"

"I dropped her at her home." His tone was not encouraging, and his aunt did not probe further, but a twinkle of satisfaction came into her bright blue eyes.

Kate, carefully mixing a salad dressing, watched sympathetically as Mrs. Butler welcomed Punch home. It was hard to tell who was the more excited of the two—the dog was breathless with delight, his tail rotating violently, and the woman was flushed and joyful.

Punch came to lay his head on Kate's knee. She washed her hands and knelt to make a fuss of him.

"You two are ruining him, you know that, don't you?" Nick was gruff, but beneath the roughness lay a warm, tender amusement.

"So you're going out with Jimmy tonight?" Nick picked up a piece of cucumber and nibbled it, watching her.

Mrs. Butler looked at them both with great interest. "Kate? Are you?"

Kate nodded, very pink. "Unless you need me here?" Her tone was half hopeful. She would have been glad of an excuse for ringing Jimmy to refuse his invitation. Pride made it impossible for her to refuse without a good reason. She would not have Nick dictating to her.

Mrs. Butler shook her head. "Certainly not—go out and enjoy yourself. Young girls should get out now and then . . ." Her blue eyes flickered over Nicholas, gently malicious.

"I'm sure Nick doesn't mind," she said.

Kate stared at the bowl of salad. She waited, her head bent, wondering what he would say.

He said nothing. After a pause made more obvious by his tense attitude, he walked out of the kitchen.

"Well," murmured his aunt in a voice choked with laughter, "Nick is in a funny mood tonight! I think he quarrelled with Sylvia over something."

Over me? thought Kate guiltily. She remembered the hostility she had noticed earlier, in the garden. Nicholas had looked at Sylvia in such an odd way. He had resented Sylvia's manner towards herself—Nick had a strong sense of fair play, and he saw Sylvia's haughty behaviour towards an employee in a very poor light.

She spent some time later in getting ready for her evening with Jimmy. When he arrived, only Nicholas and his aunt were in the kitchen, playing dominoes in a humorous atmosphere of mock hostility.

"Cheat!" Nick glared at his aunt. "Why must you always cheat?"

"I was not cheating," she said placidly. "I'm merely very absent-minded. I forgot I'd declared no two earlier."

"How could you declare it when you had a two? Cheat!"

"I overlooked this one," she said, giving him a winning smile.

Nick groaned. "Overlooked it! Do you expect me to believe that?"

Her husky voice warmed. "My dear boy, I can't help getting old and stupid, can I?"

He smiled his disbelief.

Jimmy coughed and they looked around, surprised find him standing in the kitchen door.

"I did knock, but you didn't hear me!"

Mrs. Butler grinned at him. "Goodness, you do look distinguished, Jimmy!"

Elegant in a frilled white shirt and dark lounge suit, he grinned back. "Thanks!"

Nick surveyed him without speaking, and Jimmy threw him an impudent smile. "Hi, Nick. How are you?"

"Don't forget what I said to you," Nick said menacingly. He stalked to the door and went out.

"What was all that about?" Mrs. Butler looked at the door with wide, amused eyes.

Jimmy shrugged. "Nick appears to be turning into Mr. Barratt of Wimpole Street—he talks as though Kate were his daughter, and a very young one at that. I'm hardly Attila the Hun. I've had some odd looks from fathers before now, but I've never been threatened by an employer before!"

Mrs. Butler laughed. "Nick is concerned for Kate,

She's very young, after all, and has had a sheltered upbringing."

"I'm taking her out to dinner, not kidnapping her," Jimmy said. "Nick came over to the farm this morning and breathed hell fire and damnation all over me. I resent it. My intentions are purely honourable." He grinned. "Well, more or less."

"Nick came to see you today?" Mrs. Butler stared at him in astonishment.

"You didn't know?"

"He hasn't said a word." She leaned back in her chair, blandly smiling, looking, for all her age, very regal, with her silky white coronet above those astonishingly youthful eyes.

"Nick playing the squire, perhaps?" Jimmy raised one eyebrow curiously.

"It doesn't sound like Nick, does it?"

Jimmy shrugged. "Influenced by dear Sylvia, perhaps? She certainly has a fixation about Nick being the lord of the manor."

"Nick has never shared it." Mrs. Butler was firm.

"No, I'll grant that. All the same, he did come over to see me, breathing fire, and offering to slit my throat if I harmed Kate." Jimmy laughed. "I felt quite wicked and abandoned when he'd gone—sort of rake's progress feeling. I'd never seen myself in that light before. It was faintly entrancing."

"Jimmy, you're showing off," said Mrs. Butler gently.

He grimaced. "Nick put my back up."

"What did you say to him?" She watched him

with curiosity and hidden pleasure.

Jimmy hesitated, then laughed. "I reminded him that he was in no position to talk. I remember the days when Nick was the local Don Juan. Pre-Sylvia, of course. I bet no one came and warned him off the course."

"Was Nick annoyed?" Mrs. Butler was openly amused now.

"Annoyed? He was livid! I thought he was going to push my face through the back of my head for a minute. Then he left—suddenly."

The vivid blue eyes sparkled. "How very interesting."

Jimmy looked at her with narrowed eyes. "Yes, I thought so, too." He stopped speaking as Kate entered the room, her brown hair shining silkily, full green skirts flaring round her slim legs as she walked. She looked gay and vital, smiling as she took Jimmy's outstretched hands.

"Well, hello!" Jimmy whistled. "You've done something to yourself—you look different."

"An improvement?" Her eyes laughed at him.

"Definitely," he agreed.

Mrs. Butler was wide-eyed, and Kate looked at her eagerly. "Do you like the new me?"

"Charming," Mrs. Butler nodded. "Quite charming. What a difference clothes can make! You always look very attractive, my dear, even in those jeans, but in that dress you look quite stunning . . . that is the word, wouldn't you say, Jimmy?"

"Stunning is the *mot juste*," he agreed with a grin.

Kate kissed her, on impulse. "I won't be late, I promise."

Mrs. Butler hugged her. "Forget time for tonight. Just enjoy yourself, child."

There was no sign of Nicholas as they left the house, but as they drove down the drive, Kate, glancing wistfully back, was sure she saw his head outlined against the faint gleam of a window upstairs.

"I've booked a table at my favourite restaurant." Jimmy smiled at her. "I hope you like French cooking."

"Where is it?"

"Half an hour's drive—very popular night spot. You can dance after dinner, and they do a couple of floor shows. Good band, friendly people. You'll like it."

"It sounds rather smart. Am I suitably dressed?" She looked down doubtfully.

"Perfect," he assured her. "This isn't London, you know. Girls wear almost anything to these places and no one raises an eyebrow. Things are pretty free and easy."

"Well, that's a relief." She settled back with a sigh. They drove in silence for a while, then Jimmy glanced at her and asked what she was thinking about.

"Sylvia," she said absently, then flushed and looked at him in consternation.

"Funny," he said cheerfully, "so was I! Tell me, Princess, what have you done to offend Sylvia?"

"How do you mean?" She was wary.

"When I asked her to give you the message about our date I did it as a tease. I knew it would make her mad to be used as a messenger to another girl, but I didn't expect it to have quite such an effect. She went purple with rage. She hates you, sweetie." He looked at her oddly. "I wonder why."

'You're exaggerating."

He shook his head. "No, Sylvia despises me too much to hide her feelings in front of me. She might pretend with Nick, but never with me. What have you done to her?"

"I haven't done anything." Kate spoke firmly, with some annoyance at his persistence. She did not want to continue with this conversation.

"Come off it, love. Even Sylvia isn't that irrational. I suppose she objects to Nick's interest in you?"

His calm reference to Nick brought a flood of hot, revealing colour to her face. She felt her heart thud against her chest and her throat closed convulsively.

Jimmy shot her a look. "Sorry, am I trespassing on private territory? I was just waffling. But take my advice and steer clear of Sylvia. She makes Mata Hari look like Goldilocks. She's far from being a nice girl."

"I never thought Goldilocks was very nice, either," said Kate in a desperate attempt to change the subject. "Eating other people's porridge, breaking up their home . . ."

"That does sound like Sylvia," agreed Jimmy, with a hoot of laughter.

"How is your father?" Kate asked wildly.

Jimmy laughed, but obligingly replied, and the conversation left the subject of Sylvia for the rest of the evening.

The meal was delectable, beautifully cooked and served, in pleasant but not over-obtrusive surroundings. After they had eaten they danced for a while, then watched the cabaret. Kate found herself getting tired soon afterwards. She was not used to late nights or noise, and the atmosphere of the restaurant during the floor show was rather wearing. The band was beginning to make her head ache, the dazzle of revolving lights, the overheated atmosphere, all combined to give her a feeling of sudden weariness.

Jimmy grimaced, seeing her suddenly drooping. "You look like a last year's snowdrop. Getting late for you? Shall we go?"

She smiled apologetically. "I'm sorry, it's a bore for you, but I usually go to bed so early. I think you have to be in training for one of these places."

"Don't think about it," he shrugged. "I'm usually an early bird myself. The farm work starts at crack of dawn, you know, and for all Nick's belief that I'm a gay rover, I tend to be in bed by ten most nights of the week."

Kate went to the cloakroom to fetch her coat and tidy up. As she came out again into the wide lobby of the restaurant, she saw Sylvia standing with her back to the cloakroom door, talking to the very attractive man she had seen her with in Malden on the day when she bought all her clothes.

Jimmy was standing some distance away, watching

Sylvia and her companion with curiosity.

Kate walked towards him. Just before she reached him, Sylvia and her companion went into the restaurant together.

"Well, well, well," Jimmy murmured. "I wonder what that means . . ."

She looked at him enquiringly.

He grinned. "Sylvia's escort is none other than Sir Rodney Paton."

"Paton?" The name was faintly familiar. She looked into the restaurant. Sylvia and her companion had a table beside a brilliant bank of flowers. Above the pinks and purples of the flowers, Sylvia's utterly simple white dress had a classic simplicity, giving her blonde beauty a new dimension. The finely pleated white folds moulded her body. Around her throat hung a silver chain from which an emerald glittered, set in heavy antique silver. Her hair was swathed elegantly above her face and pinned with a silver lover's knot. She smiled at her companion, leaning forward so that the emerald shone at him as brightly as her green eyes, the cold stone lying just above the fullness of her white breasts.

Jimmy whistled beneath his breath. "Boy, is he hooked! Sylvia has a problem."

Kate looked at him with puzzled, worried eyes, her brow knit in concern.

"Rodney Paton is the big electronics king. Three factories in the south of England, a house in London, and a very elegant house here in Essex. He's a millionaire—just what Sylvia has always wanted for her birthday."

"Oh," said Kate softly, her frown deepening.

"Oh, indeed," Jimmy echoed. "But what will dear Sylvia do about Nick? Sir Rodney may be stinking rich, but he isn't either as young or as good-looking as Nick. I imagine Sylvia is wishing she could have her cake and eat it."

Kate looked at the man who sat opposite Sylvia. He had a charming, attentive smile on his face, and she could see, even at this distance, that Sylvia engrossed all his attention. He was, as Jimmy had put it, quite hooked. His eyes flickered now and then, tracing the proud sweep of Sylvia's body in the white dress. Then he looked up into her green eyes, and his smile deepened.

Sylvia was more difficult to read. She was totally responsive to her companion, her eyes fixed on his, her manner pliant and quietly eager, vaguely little-girl beneath her sophistication.

Kate already knew her too well to be deceived. Sylvia, like a first-rate actress, was giving the performance of her life, but for all its brilliance, it was still acting, and the hollowness came over to the other girl very clearly.

"She isn't in love with him," she said aloud.

Jimmy laughed. "Simple Kate! Bless you, of course not. How could you think it?"

"But she is in love with Nick," Kate said falteringly, and with reluctance. Then, because she had to be honest with herself, "Or rather, she wants more from Nick than just his money. Nick himself attracts her."

"Sex is a powerful attraction, Kate," Jimmy said lightly. "Even Sylvia has to weigh that against money. When money and sex come in the same box it's very tempting." He put an arm around her and led her out of the restaurant. "Cheer up! Sir Rodney may not be as sexy as Nick, but he has a damned sight more money."

"It's nothing to do with me," she said defiantly.

Jimmy sighed. "Dear Kate, I'm on your side, you know. I have a grievance against Sylvia."

"Oh?" She let him help her into the car and looked up at him as he shut the door.

"Sylvia has consistently ignored me," he said, grinning. "That's a deadly insult to my virility."

She laughed at that, smiling at him as he slid the car into reverse and backed out of the car park. "Sylvia doesn't know what she's missed," she said.

He was amused. "Don't let Nick hear you say that!"

"Nick?" She was flushed again at once. "Why shouldn't I?" Her chin went up in defiance.

"I'm beginning to wonder," Jimmy said softly.

CHAPTER SEVEN

IT was midnight when Jimmy drove back through the gates of Sanctuary. The wind made restless music in the trees which lined the drive. A few stars sparkled faintly in the sky. Kate was too sleepy to feel more than a faint interest as the dark bulk of the house drew nearer. All the lights were out. She had expected that, since Mrs. Butler went to bed very early, but she knew that the kitchen door was always unlocked. Country habits were different from town ones. No burglar would be attracted to Sanctuary—the loneliness and isolation meant that he would need a vehicle, and the dogs which slept in the kitchen at night, friendly though they were, would be sufficient warning of intruders.

Jimmy Whitney was a countryman, and knew that he would find an unlocked door at the back of the house, so drove round to the stable yard to let her out of the car. He walked to the kitchen door with her. They were both relaxed and at ease. It had been an enjoyable evening. Wine, music and dancing had made them closer to each other than any other entertainment would have done.

There was something, Kate decided, about dancing that made it easier to relax. The combination of exercise and pleasure, perhaps. She yawned and Jimmy laughed.

"You won't need a cup of cocoa before bed tonight!"

"Would you like one?"

He shook his head. "Better not—Nick might suspect I was seducing you down here!"

This made her immediately determinedly rebellious. "I shall make some for myself. You might as well have some. Blow Nick."

Jimmy laughed. "All right—if you want to play it that way. Blow Nick indeed!"

She made cocoa in a small saucepan while Jimmy lounged against the table, talking in a soft voice so as not to disturb the house. The dogs, having given them an excited but subdued welcome, had gone back to sleep in various corners.

"It was fun tonight, wasn't it?" Jimmy smiled reminiscently. "I had a fantastic evening. I hope you did."

"You know I did," she said indulgently. "I've never in my life been to a place like that. It was all so new to me."

"We'll go again," he promised.

"I must buy a more suitable dress," she said. "And silver shoes, like that girl I pointed out to you."

She poured out the cocoa and set a mug in front of him. Jimmy smiled at her.

"You looked much more attractive than that girl! Clothes don't matter that much."

"Dancing does," she said. "I ought to learn to dance properly."

"You picked it up quickly enough! You're a natural dancer." He slid an arm around her and hummed under his breath. Kate laughed, swaying against him, her hand resting on his shoulder.

Jimmy spun her in a dramatic swirl, and came up short against the wall. He laughed down into her upturned face. "You're fantastic, Kate!"

A voice made them both jump. "What the hell do you think you're doing at this time of night?"

Nick, ruffled of hair and glowering of countenance, stood in the doorway, his dressing-gown loosely belted over wine-coloured pyjamas.

Jimmy's hands dropped from her like lead. "Oh, hello, Nick," he said. "I'm just going. Good night, Kate."

Kate turned, hasty words on her lips, but he had already gone, sliding out of the door in a second.

She stood, wondering what to do. Should she go up to bed, like a scolded schoolgirl, or defy Nick, stay here and drink her cocoa? She decided to do the latter. Lifting her chin in defiance, she went to the table, picked up her mug and sipped.

Nick stared at her grimly. "All my warnings went over your head, didn't they?"

"I like Jimmy," she flung back. "So he flirts! Maybe I flirt, too! Had you thought of that? Girls can flirt, you know, without being scarlet women!"

He laughed. "You flirt? Don't be ridiculous!"

She looked at him from under her lashes, deliberately provocative. "You think I couldn't?"

He strolled forward. Her heart began to thud and

her mouth was suddenly dry.

"Don't throw down the gauntlet to me," he said softly. "I just might pick it up."

She wanted to retort in a casual manner, but the words seemed to be jammed in her throat. He stood too close. He was too overpowering. She felt suddenly weak, afraid of self-betrayal.

He laughed. "I thought you'd change your mind!" Then he drew back, picked up the mug of cocoa she had made for Jimmy. "I might as well drink this—no point in wasting good milk." He drank a little, then looked gently at her over the rim. "I'm not playing the heavy father for my own fun, you know. You're very ignorant of the man-woman relationship, Jimmy Whitney, whatever you may imagine, is an expert. I only wanted to save you a nasty experience."

"Do you think we any of us learn from other people's experience? Don't we only learn from our own?"

He sighed. "Very well, if you insist on playing with fire, go ahead." He looked weary and drawn. He put down the cocoa and walked to the door. Kate wanted to run after him, promise never to see Jimmy again, but she knew that she must not do that. Better for Nick to disapprove of her because she went out with Jimmy than for him ever to suspect that she was in love with himself.

She finished her cocoa, washed up the two mugs and left them to drain on the draining-board. The dogs lifted lazy heads in farewell as she went to the door. She snapped out the light and left them to sleep peacefully until morning.

During the night Kate woke several times, hearing faint coughing, and sat up to listen with a frown. It was hard to slide back into sleep, and, weary as she was, she felt uneasy. It could not be Nick coughing. Was it Mrs. Butler?

At last she got out of bed, slipped into her dressing-gown and padded along to the older woman's bedroom.

Her knock was answered immediately. A husky voice said, "Come in, my dear . . ."

Mrs. Butler was sitting up in her bed, the bedside lamp shedding a pale halo around her. Her white hair hung in plaits beside her face. In the white flannelette nightgown she looked oddly like a schoolgirl.

"I heard someone coughing. Are you ill?" Kate looked at her in concern. Surely her face was very flushed?

"I think I've developed a cold . . ." The voice whispered drily, like a reed blown by the wind.

Kate bent over her, touched her forehead. It was dry and very hot. Her cheeks were hot, too. The crumpled skin felt rougher than usual. A pulse beat visibly at the base of the thin neck, in a deep hollow above the tiny lace frill of the nightgown.

"You are a little hot," Kate said slowly. "Running a slight temperature. A touch of 'flu, perhaps. It's just the weather for it—a deceptive thaw in spring is always the time when one catches a cold."

"I shall be all right," Mrs. Butler said, and then

was shaken by another bout of coughing, bending forward, her slight body at the mercy of the cough.

"You must be good," Kate said firmly. "Stay in bed until that cough has gone."

"Stay in bed?" Mrs. Butler laughed. "Nonsense! I'm not a baby to be mollycoddled like that!"

"If you neglect a cold it can turn into something much worse," Kate threatened. "You don't want to be ill, do you? Much better to take precautions."

"Mollycoddling!" snorted Mrs. Butler.

"No such thing. Just being sensible. I'll bring you your meals in bed."

"You'll do no such thing! This isn't a hospital!"

"It will be no trouble to me. And I can cook for Nick, too. Mrs. Pepper will be doing all the housework as usual. Nick won't mind."

Mrs. Butler was silent, her bright blue eyes gazing at the opposite wall in a trance-like stare. Then she smiled. "Very well, child. If you insist! If you're sure you can manage Nick."

"Of course I can manage Nick!" Then Kate stood still, looking down at the old woman with suspicious eyes. Mrs. Butler met her glance innocently enough, but what was that at the back of the amazingly clear, vivid eyes? Kate was undecided. Then Mrs. Butler smiled up at her sleepily.

"I hate to trouble you, my dear, but my throat is so dry . . ."

"Hot milk," Kate nodded, and turned to hurry down to the kitchen.

She returned in a few moments with a glass of

warm milk, flavoured with a tiny sprinkling of nutmeg and some sugar. Mrs. Butler took it gratefully, sipped and beamed at her. "Delicious!" She finished the drink in a moment. Kate shook out her pillows and helped her to settle more comfortably.

"Try not to lie on your back. Your cough will be easier if you remember that." She tucked her in gently, smiling at her, and turned out the light.

"Goodnight, my dear," murmured Mrs. Butler. Kate tiptoed to the door and went out.

Nick was leaning in the passage, his brow stern. She gasped at the sight of him and put a finger to her lips. He followed her down to her own room. She turned, on the threshold, and looked at him.

"Your aunt isn't very well," she told him.

"What is the matter with her? Why didn't you wake me?"

She explained, and he listened in some concern. "Is it serious, do you think?"

Kate shook her head. "I'm sure not, but it's best to be quite certain. She's agreed to stay in bed for a few days."

He raised an eyebrow. "Doesn't sound like Aunt Elaine! She's usually dead against any such idea! She must be worse than you think. We must get the doctor first thing in the morning."

"I agree," she nodded. "Goodnight."

He stood, staring at her closed door for a moment, then stalked back to his own room without answering.

The doctor was reassuring after he had seen his patient,

"She'll do," he told them cheerfully. "I wish all my patients were as active as she is—she puts most of them in the shade."

"Is it just a cold?" Nicholas asked him.

He played vaguely with the stethoscope hanging from his neck. "Well, perhaps a little more than that."

Kate noticed that his eyes slid away as he spoke, and she immediately suspected him of conspiring with Aunt Elaine. "Influenza?" she asked abruptly.

He glanced at her. "I'm not certain. I'll be back to see her tomorrow. Keep her in bed for the time being. Be firm about it. She can be obstinate, I know, but at her age it's not wise to neglect a bad cough."

When he had gone Nicholas leaned against the kitchen table, watching Kate preparing a light lunch for his aunt. "Are you worried about her?" His voice was tense, and she glanced at him in surprise.

"No, of course not. You heard the doctor."

"He sounded serious to me," he said, frowning. "It isn't like him to fuss, or like Aunt Elaine to be so ready to put up with fuss."

Kate lifted the tray, checking that it was properly set. She had added a slender glass vase containing one fragrant spray of lilac. Salad and a little grilled fish, bread and butter and a small bowl of fruit.

"She won't eat the fish," Nick said absently.

"I'll take that risk," she answered, moving towards the door. He took the tray from her and gestured.

"I'll take this up. I want a word with her. Have we got the same? Will it spoil if I stay up with her for a little while? I'm beginning to think it's time I had a long talk with Aunt Elaine."

"We've got roast lamb," she said. "It isn't ready yet, so you have plenty of time. I'll call you when it's on the table."

"Call me before that," he said. "I don't like cold food."

Kate glared at the door, feeling like throwing something after him, then turned towards the oven to check the condition of the lamb. It was browning nicely. Mrs. Pepper would not, of course, be coming today, since it was Sunday, and she had plenty to occupy her while Nick was upstairs with his aunt, but Kate could not help being very curious about their long conversation. The hands of the clock crept round. The meal was almost ready, but still Nick did not come downstairs. What could they be discussing? He had looked ominous when he left the kitchen. Had he, too, suspected that his aunt was to a certain extent exaggerating her illness in order to throw them even closer together?

Kate had begun to suspect it last night. Mrs. Butler had not seemed ready to stay in bed until it occurred to her that, with herself out of the way, Nick and Kate would be spending the Sunday alone in the house, to all intents and purposes. A long, quiet day with no other visitors expected.

Kate sighed. Her hand brushed a curling tendril of hair back from her flushed forehead as she bent over the roast lamb. The meat was beautifully cooked, the vegetables nearing perfection. She had made the rich, brown gravy and the mint sauce was standing on the table in a sauceboat.

She called Nick, and a moment later he came downstairs with the tray. Mrs. Butler had eaten the salad and picked a little at the fish.

"She said it was delicious, but her appetite seemed very small," he said, seeing her eyes on the fish.

"You . . . you weren't upsetting her?"

The grey eyes were cold as winter frost. "Why should I be?"

Kate defied the grey eyes, her chin rebellious. "You seem to be in something of a temper to me! You were up there a long time, and I suspect you were arguing with her."

"I don't really think that's any of your business," Nicholas said icily.

She flushed, but stuck to her guns. "Maybe not, but I feel responsible for Aunt Elaine . . ."

"You call her that now, do you?" His tone cracked like a whip.

"She asked me to," she retorted. "You were in the room at the time!"

"I don't recall it," he said dismissively, leaving a lingering implication that she lied.

Fiery-eyed, she snapped, "Ask her, then!"

"Oh, she'll support you. She seems infatuated with you! She wants everyone else to be so, too, but we're not all as gullible and emotional as Aunt Elaine!"

She went white. He had brought it out into the open at last, and the cruelly biting contempt of his voice was gall and wormwood to her. She straightened herself, head held high, facing him with wide, hurt eyes.

"I don't know what your aunt wants, but for myself I want nothing whatever!"

He laughed, his lip curling. "You expect me to believe that? Sylvia's right—you showed from the first day how you felt about Sanctuary. It's a lovely house, I can understand your attraction towards it. But you must get used to the fact that you'll only be living here for a short time."

Drily, she whispered, "What are you really saying, Mr. Adams?"

His voice was rough. "Don't put down roots, Kate. You don't belong here. You never can."

She nodded. "I know that. Your aunt may have some crazy ideas about the way things are, but I can assure you that I don't agree with her. Not in the least. I . . . I'm ready to leave whenever it's desirable."

He turned away. "That might be now," he said in that brutal, rough tone.

She shrugged. The back of her throat stung with salt. Her eyes were dry, though, and she kept her chin up. "I'm ready," she said.

He was silent for an instant, then he said in a calm voice, "No, perhaps we had better wait until Aunt Elaine is better. She needs you here for the moment." His gaze swung back to her, shifted slightly as it met her own. "I have never known her take such a fancy to anyone," he said abruptly.

"I'm glad she likes me. I like her."

He nodded. "You're a kind girl. You'll know how to help her over the difficult days. She must be made to accept Sylvia—that's all we can hope for now. You can do it if you really want to . . ." Again the grey eyes stabbed at her accusingly.

"I'll do what I can," she said flatly.

"The best you can?" he challenged.

"Do you think I want her to . . ." The hot, angry words trailed off, and Kate bit her lower lip. "I'll do my best," she finished.

The meal was almost silent. Now and then she looked up to find Nicholas staring at her. He would look away, and she would choke back a painful sigh.

It was a bitter thought that he suspected her of plotting with his aunt to exclude Sylvia from Sanctuary. A bitter thought that he believed her to be laying traps for him! Humiliation and pain made her wince at the idea. For the moment he seemed to think her mercenary in her supposed plan to steal his affections from Sylvia. That, at least, was preferable to the truth—she could not have borne it if he had guessed that she was in love with him. Any suspicion, dislike or scorn was better than the real truth.

When she took Mrs. Butler a tray of afternoon tea later, she found her dozing gently, an open book in front of her on the neat coverlet.

Opening one eye, the old woman gazed at her. "You look very mutinous! Has Nick been saying things?"

"He said enough," Kate told her. "What did you say to him, that's more the question!"

An impish smile hovered around the old mouth

and a twinkle lit the vivid blue eyes. "Didn't he tell you?"

"He did not!"

"Then why should I? Presumably he prefers to keep it quiet, and I don't blame him!"

Kate sat down on the side of the bed and stared at her in some bewilderment. "Are we talking about the same thing?"

"We're talking about the fact that Nick no longer loves Sylvia," triumphed Mrs. Butler.

Kate felt the colour rush from her cheeks. She swallowed and her ears went oddly deaf, then her eyes focused on the flushed old face.

"Did he actually tell you so?" she demanded.

Mrs. Butler shrugged. "He didn't tell me so in so many words, but the whole tone of the discussion made it very clear. No man in love would talk about his girl in those terms!"

"You're evading the issue," said Kate certainly. "From what he said to me I came into the discussion somewhere, and Nick now has the impression that I've been plotting to . . ." Her voice died, she was suddenly scarlet.

"To what?" asked Mrs. Butler teasingly.

Kate got up hurriedly. "Enjoy your tea," she said, and left the room. She had meant to have it out with the old lady, but somehow she just could not bring herself to do it. It would be far too embarrassing, and the fact that she could sense Mrs. Butler's amusement underlying what they had already said made her even more shy.

She could hear Nicholas talking to the dogs in the kitchen. She stood, hesitating, wondering what to do, and was relieved when the telephone rang in the office. It was Jimmy, suggesting a drive to have tea at the farm, and she did not need time to consider his invitation. It would take her out of Nick's company, and that was enough.

Nick appeared very angry when she informed him that she was going out with Jimmy, but he said nothing at all, merely nodded curtly. The back of his neck was suddenly dark red, though, and she saw his mouth tighten as he turned away.

"Will you tell your aunt?" she asked nervously when she came into the kitchen a moment later in one of her new skirts, the calf-length black one, teamed with the green crêpe blouse.

"Afraid to do so?" he derided, his eyes skimming over her without a change in his grim expression.

"She's probably asleep," she excused. "I don't want to wake her for no good reason."

He shrugged. "Oh, very well, I'll tell her. What about my supper?"

"Cold meat and salad," she said, indicating the refrigerator.

"It won't work, you know," he said suddenly.

She was confused. "What won't work?"

"I'm not going to be stung into a display of jealousy!"

She was very still, her face crimson, her legs trembling so much that she wanted to sit down. In a hoarse, alien voice, she said, "What are you talking about?"

and laughed. It was a weak, rather self-conscious little laugh, but it had a decided effect.

Nicholas gave her a furious look and stalked out of the room, slamming the door behind him with a bang that made her ears buzz horribly for a full minute afterwards.

Kate put her hands to her hot face and groaned. "I wish I'd never come to this house! I wish I'd never set eyes on any of them!"

CHAPTER EIGHT

NEXT morning, after feeding the animals and milking the goats, Kate took Mrs. Butler up some breakfast on a tray, and found the old lady sitting up in her bed with a grim expression on her face.

The curtains were drawn, a window wide open. The fresh, cool morning air blew in across the room.

"You shouldn't have got out of bed," Kate scolded, putting the tray down on the bedside table and rushing round the bed to close the window. "And you shouldn't have windows open when you've got 'flu."

"Why did you go out with Jimmy Whitney again last night?" Mrs. Butler's voice was brusque and tinged with challenge.

Kate came back to the bedside and gently pulled the covers up, smoothed the tumbled pillows. She placed the tray on the bed in front of Mrs. Butler.

"You are going to eat this, aren't you? You must eat something this morning."

Mrs. Butler looked at the carefully arranged tray. There was a boiled egg, under a knitted cosy; a small china pot of tea and a glass of orange juice. Slender fingers of thin bread and butter, a pot of marmalade and a delicate flower-painted porcelain cup. In a tiny matching vase Kate had arranged some primroses with the dew on their golden centres.

With a sigh, the old woman pushed the tray away. "Kate, why did you go out with Jimmy last night? Why didn't you stay at home here?"

"You know why," Kate said quietly.

"Your scruples are ridiculous, my dear," said Mrs. Butler.

"Please eat something . . . some bread and butter?" Kate sat down on the edge of the bed and picked up the glass of orange juice. As though she were feeding a child she held the glass to the tired old mouth. Mrs. Butler obediently sipped.

When she had drunk most of the juice Kate began to feed her with the bread and butter. Mrs. Butler complained weakly, but did not push the food away. She even allowed Kate to feed her with some of the egg. Then Kate poured her some tea, and sat down to watch her drink it from a chair beside the bed.

"Nick wants me to leave here," Kate said at last. "He was very angry with both of us yesterday. I think he's right—I should go."

"Not yet," Mrs. Butler pleaded. "Promise to stay for a little while. I need you." She lay back against the pillows with a gesture of weariness. "I feel so tired, Kate."

Kate was alarmed. She put one hand to the pulse which beat at the base of Mrs. Butler's throat. The pulse was almost indefinable. She gently encircled the thin wrist. Here again, the pulse beat slow and faint. There was no colour in Mrs. Butler's face. Her eyes were dimmed, as though the vivid flash of their blue had been dowsed by illness.

"I'll call the doctor again," said Kate, getting up. She took the tray downstairs and rang the doctor. He sounded concerned when she mentioned the weakness of Mrs. Butler's pulse, and promised to come as soon as he could.

"Make her rest. Has she eaten?"

"Very little. I was worried about it."

"Don't force her to eat. If she's ill she'll lose her appetite. Best not to force her."

Kate went back upstairs and found Mrs. Butler almost asleep, her lids lowered over the blue eyes, her hands lying on the coverlet in relaxed repose. The thin, fragile lids rose. The blue eyes looked gently at Kate.

"Promise . . ." The whisper came so faintly that Kate had to bend to her to hear what she said.

Kate understood her. She put a hand over one of the delicate hands on the coverlet. "I promise," she said gently.

The fingers trembled, then were still. Kate watched and heard the breathing become regular, the features composed. When she was certain that Mrs. Butler was asleep she stole gently away, leaving the door open so that she could hear if she was called.

She found Mrs. Pepper busy downstairs, and explained to her about Mrs. Butler's illness. Mrs. Pepper was very upset.

"Oh, dear, poor old thing! And she's so healthy, as a rule. I hope it's nothing worse than a touch of 'flu. At that age they can pop off as quick as a candle blowing out."

"Don't!" Kate's voice was harsh. She stiffened, half angry, half terrified.

Mrs. Pepper looked at her in surprise. "I'm sorry, dear, I was just speaking aloud."

Kate was very pale. "I'm sorry if I spoke abruptly. I've got very fond of Mrs. Butler."

"She's a bit cantankerous over some things," Mrs. Pepper said thoughtfully. "But there's something about her, all right. She's like this house—quality. It tells, doesn't it?"

Kate looked at the warm, sunlit kitchen. "Yes," she said slowly. "Quality tells."

"Lucky she's got you to look after her animals," Mrs. Pepper said. "She'd be worrying if she hadn't." After a silent pause, she asked, "Have you rung Mr. Nick?"

"He knows she has 'flu," Kate said tautly.

"I'm surprised he went to work, then. Very fond of his aunt, he is, very fond."

Kate thought about what Mrs. Pepper had said for the rest of that long, anxious day. The doctor came and pronounced Mrs. Butler to be distinctly worse. She was now very flushed, heavily sleepy and fighting for breath.

"Her lungs are very congested. I'll give you something for that. It will help a little, but there's not really much I can do at this stage. It must run its course."

"She sounds so ill now—her breathing is frightening."

The doctor stood beside the bed, watching Mrs. Butler's face with a little frown. "Yes, but I hope that

that will clear a little later today. The main thing is that her heart is sound enough to cope with this additional strain."

"Is her heart sound?" Kate studied his eyes as he replied to her anxious question.

He looked uncertain for a second or two, then he said slowly, "I hope so."

She would have pressed the matter further, but he turned away and began to write out a prescription. His writing was totally indecipherable, a toppling scrawl that baffled the keenest eyes. He tore the sheet off the pad and handed it to her.

"Have this made up at once!"

As he picked up his bag and departed Kate followed him down the stairs. At the foot she caught at his sleeve and looked up into his face.

"I'm here alone. I can't leave her. Should I ring Nick and get him to come home to fetch the prescription?"

"Yes, I should do that!" He nodded, not unkindly, and walked towards the front door. She let him out and stood nervously, staring at nothing, in the musty gloom of the hall.

Nick's secretary was sympathetic, when she rang his office, but unable to be of much help.

"He isn't here."

"Oh, dear!" Kate was distracted with worry. "Do you know when he'll be back? Where I could get in touch with him?"

"Is it urgent?" The girl was curious.

"Very urgent. His aunt is ill. He's needed here."

The girl hesitated. "I don't actually know where he is, you see—he didn't say where he was going. But he drove past here an hour ago with his fiancée in the passenger seat, so he might be at her place."

Kate swallowed on a wave of pain and sick jealousy. "I see. Thank you, I'll try her. Have you got her number?"

The girl gave it to her. Kate wrote the number on the top of the telephone directory in a wavering scrawl. She stood for a long moment, staring at the now silent telephone, then forced herself to pick up the receiver.

Sylvia answered, her voice clear and holding a hint of cold irritation.

"Is Nick there?" Kate was so nervous that she spoke abruptly. There was a little silence at the other end.

Then Sylvia said curtly, "No," and slammed the telephone down with a crash that made Kate's ear reverberate for minutes on end.

What should she do now? She must get someone to collect the prescription which the doctor had said must reach Mrs. Butler as soon as possible, yet she dared not leave the house. Mrs. Butler needed constant attention. Every moment in which she was left alone was a dangerous moment. Kate stood, biting her lip, staring around her in absolute panic.

Then she pulled herself together. Jimmy! A smile of relief touched her mouth and she ran to the telephone again.

Jimmy was, luckily, in the house when she rang,

and when she explained her dilemma was cheerfully willing to do whatever he could to help.

"Glad to do anything! I'll be there in five minutes. Keep cheerful!" He rang off, and she stood for a second longer, feeling the relief welling up inside her chest.

She ran upstairs to check on Mrs. Butler's condition, and was delighted to find her sleeping deeply. Her face was very flushed, her breathing choked, but after Kate's recent alarms the old lady's real condition was in a way a faint relief. Kate had been imagining her to be much worse than this, and although she was still very anxious, she now felt more confident as she returned to the kitchen to wait for Jimmy.

She made a large jug of cold lemonade, added ice and a packet of straws and put them all on a tray, to take them upstairs to Mrs. Butler later.

Jimmy arrived soon after she had completed these preparations. She gave him the prescription, thanking him again for his help.

"Think nothing of it! I'm glad to do anything I can. What are neighbours for, after all? When she's better, you can come over and cook a meal for Dad and myself. That will make the old man really happy. He asked me to tell you that if you need a sick nurse he's willing to come over and sit with Mrs. Butler for a few hours. He says it's quite respectable because he's known her for so long."

"That was very kind of him," she smiled. "I'm sure Mrs. Butler would be touched if she knew."

Jimmy looked at her soberly. "Is she very ill? I can't

believe it! Aunt Elaine has always seemed so strong—I can't remember her having a day's illness before."

"She looks ill," Kate said slowly. "But I can't be sure just how bad it is—the doctor is very non-committal. You know what they can be like. He says very little, but I thought he looked worried when he was here last. At her age it's so hard to say. It's the same with children. They can look as if they're at death's door, yet be up and about in twenty-four hours."

Jimmy watched her closely. "Does Aunt Elaine look as if she's at death's door?"

Kate hesitated, then nodded in silence. Jimmy, equally silently, patted her shoulder.

"I'll be back with this prescription in half an hour or so. I'll have to drive into town to pick it up. The only dispensing chemist for miles around, you know. Disgraceful, isn't it?"

When he had gone, Kate went upstairs to the bedroom with her tray. She had made herself a cup of coffee. She sat down beside Aunt Elaine, settled herself and drank her coffee slowly. Once she had made certain that the old lady was still deeply asleep, she began to read the book she had brought up, a collection of short stories. Her mind could not concentrate, however. Her thoughts kept wandering. Each tiny alteration in her companion's breathing made her sit up, alert and anxious. Mrs. Butler appeared to be slowly getting worse. Or, she wondered, was that only her anxiety playing tricks on her?

If only I knew more about nursing, Kate thought

unhappily. She had nursed her aunt, but that had been a totally different illness, a long, unchanging condition which had given her no sudden crisis to cope with.

Once the congested lungs brought about a fit of violent coughing. Kate hurriedly helped Mrs. Butler to sit up, supporting her gently. Then she gave her some lemonade to sip, once the coughing had stopped, and Mrs. Butler drank thirstily.

As Kate laid her down again, propped up on pillows, the fragile lids rose and the blue eyes flashed into focus.

"Kate . . ." The thready voice was almost inaudible, and she bent to catch the words. "Kate, thank you . . ." Husky, panted out, the words brought tears to her eyes.

Kate smiled, "Silly!"

Mrs. Butler sketched an answering smile, weak, wavering, full of affection.

The pattern was laid down. When Jimmy came quietly up the stairs and brought the medicine prescribed by the doctor, he found Kate again supporting the old lady, offering her another drink of lemonade. Jimmy stood, watching them in silence. When Kate had laid Mrs. Butler down again, she turned her head to smile at him.

"You were quicker than I'd dared hope!"

He came across the room and gave her the package. "How is she? She looks terrible." He spoke softly, so as not to disturb the patient, but Kate looked at her in alarm, then shook her head at Jimmy in warning.

She tiptoed across the room, and he followed her.

On the landing she smiled at him.

"Sorry, but I don't want to frighten her. Confidence can be very important in an illness."

"I'm sorry," he corrected her. "It was a dumb thing to say. I just assumed that she was past hearing me. She looks as if only a bomb would bring her out of it."

Kate frowned. "She is very ill, yes. I wish I could get hold of Nick."

"Tried his office?"

She looked at him in wry amusement, and he grimaced. "Of course," he said. "Stupid of me! He wasn't there? Didn't they know where he was?"

"They thought he was at Sylvia's, but when I rang, Sylvia said he wasn't there."

"I expect he'll ring as soon as he hears you've been asking for him." Jimmy looked at her sharply. "You think Aunt Elaine is that bad, then? Bad enough for it to be a matter of urgency to find Nick?"

Kate shrugged helplessly. "I can't be certain. The doctor is no help. I can only go on what I feel—and I feel worried."

"I can see you do," Jimmy murmured. "Is there anything else I can do to help? Have you eaten since breakfast?"

She looked at him in complete astonishment. "Eaten?" Then she gasped as he showed her his watch. "Is that the time? Good heavens. I had no idea!"

"You forgot to have lunch?"

"I'd forgotten there was such a meal," she laughed. "Are you hungry?"

Her stomach answered her, suddenly violently aware of the long gap between meals, and she groaned.

"Starving, it appears."

"Stay with Aunt Elaine. I'll get us both a scratch meal. Do you like omelettes? I can do a decent omelette."

"I love them!"

"Right—two omelettes coming up!" He grinned, patted her cheek and said softly, "Stop looking so anxious. Go back in there and watch her, but look cheerful. If she sees you with a face like that she'll think her days really are numbered."

Kate mustered a smile and obeyed him. By the time he returned to the bedroom with a tray she had fed Aunt Elaine with the cool lemonade several times, and she fancied that there was a faint but distinct change for the better.

"Her temperature seems to be breaking. She's perspired since the last drink I gave her—the liquid and the aspirins are having an effect."

"Have you given her some of the medicine, too?"

She nodded, then took the tray he handed her and admired his handiwork.

He had created a beautifully golden-brown omelette, out of which tomatoes peeped at one side, and had heaped her plate with crisp fresh salad, too. Thin bread and butter, and an apple, with some fresh coffee, completed the meal.

"Jimmy, you've missed your vocation—you're a born cook!"

He grinned. "Eat the omelette while it's hot. I'll

be downstairs if you want me. I rang my father and told him I'd be here until Nick got back, so don't worry about anything. I'll be permanently on call while you need me."

She looked at him in gratitude. "This is really very sweet of you, Jimmy. I don't know what to say."

"Don't say anything. Glad to be of help." He left hurriedly, looking embarrassed.

The long hours dragged by, the afternoon drew towards evening, and still Nick did not come home. Kate once or twice wondered if she should ring his office again, but she hesitated to do so now that Mrs. Butler was showing signs of some improvement. Nick would think she had panicked unnecessarily.

After his brutal remarks about her intentions towards Sanctuary, she certainly did not want to give him any grounds for believing that she was still pursuing him. Her pride stung too bitterly for that.

At six o'clock, Jimmy insisted on relieving her at her post for half an hour, at least, and she left him in the bedroom watching Mrs. Butler while she freshened up in the bathroom and then went to the kitchen to prepare an evening meal.

Jimmy had taken care of the animals for her. The dogs surged out from their usual corners to greet her ecstatically as she entered, their greeting more excited than ever after the long quiet day during which they had sensed, with their keen intuition about atmosphere, the strain which had infected the whole house. She could tell from their darting looks at the doors, their little whines of query, that they were disturbed by Mrs. Butler's unusual absence.

"There isn't much we can hide from you, is there?" She rubbed Punch's ears, and he grew dreamy-eyed with pleasure. "Did Jimmy give you your dinner?"

"What's Jimmy doing here?" The terse question made her swing round in astonishment. Nicholas stood in the doorway, his brow stormy.

"Oh, Nick, there you are!" Relief at the sight of him made her babble. "I wondered when you would get here . . . I thought you'd disappeared off the face of the earth . . ."

"I asked you a question. What's Jimmy Whitney doing here? I just saw his face at a window upstairs."

"Mrs. Butler's window, probably," she said, her own tone becoming sharp in response to the harshness in his.

He shot her a dark look. "Aunt Elaine's room?" Then his eyes widened. "What the devil is he doing up there?" His face changed. "Is she worse? What's wrong—why didn't you let me know she was worse? Why didn't you ring me?"

"I did!" His attitude had hurt, and she snapped back.

He gave her an angry look and moved towards the other door. She caught at his arm.

"You can't go up there looking like a thundercloud. Wait a moment and try to look cheerful."

He looked down at her hand, resting on his arm. "Yes, Sister. Certainly, Sister." His voice had altered, grown lighter, had a tinge of amusement in it. "Very dictatorial all of a sudden, aren't we?"

She let her hand drop, moving back from him. "I'm sorry. I just wanted to make sure you didn't upset her."

"Well, how is she? And if you rang me, why didn't I hear about it?"

"She's been ill today, but she's slightly better now. I rang you earlier because I was rather more worried then, but you were out. I rang Sylvia, but you'd left her, too, apparently. Your office knew I was looking for you, though."

"I wasn't told." His frown boded no good for his secretary. "I was only out for an hour. Why didn't you ring again?"

She flushed. "I would have done, but I thought they would be certain to tell you I'd rung. I explained the situation."

"We had a bit of a flap this afternoon. I suppose it slipped her mind. She's fluffy-headed at the best of times." He gave her a long look. "You're pale yourself. You look exhausted. Have you been run off your feet?"

Kate shook her head. "I've been sitting down all day, watching Mrs. Butler. Her temperature was very high, but it's come down a little now."

"I'll go up now," he said. "Don't worry, I'll be bright and cheerful. I'll send Jimmy down. He came to hold your hand, did he?"

Her face grew suddenly pink. "He came to help in an emergency," she said angrily. "I needed someone to fetch the prescription which the doctor left. That was why I rang you originally. You weren't there, and I had no choice but to ask Jimmy for help." She flung him a furious look. "Which he gave willingly! He's been here ever since. He cooked my lunch and he's taken over with your aunt so that I can have a short break. I'm very grateful to him."

He grimaced. "Noble Jimmy! Don't sound so defiant, Kate. You're quite right—Jimmy has been a Trojan. I'm out of line. I'll remember to thank him, don't worry."

"Don't be so sarcastic," she snapped.

"I wasn't being sarcastic!" Nick looked surprised. "I'm sorry if it sounded like sarcasm."

She eyed him furiously. He gave her a bright, faintly mocking smile and drifted out of the room. She turned her attention to the meal which she had been preparing. A mixed grill would be the easiest meal in the circumstances. She looked into the fridge and found bacon, sausages, some steak. With mushrooms and tomatoes, she thought, that would make a very acceptable meal.

Jimmy appeared, smiling. "I'll shoot off now, if it's all the same to you. You'll have Nick as a backstop now."

"I was just going to make some supper. Will you stay and have a mixed grill?"

He grinned reluctantly. "I'd love to, but the old man will want me to help him with the usual evening jobs. I'll ring you tomorrow. If you need me, just shout." He came and kissed her lightly on the cheek. "You're an angel. Did you know that?"

She smiled. "That makes us twins, then. I was just

about to say the same thing to you. I'm very grateful for your help, Jimmy. I don't know what I would have done without you."

He hugged her and went. Kate got on with the cooking. Nicholas came into the kitchen ten minutes later, and lounged in the doorway, watching her. She avoided his gaze, but she was deeply aware of his presence. His stare made her feel uneasy.

At last she glanced at him crossly. "Is Aunt Elaine all right alone? Shall I go up and sit with her?"

"She doesn't need permanent nursing now. She spoke quite rationally to me, and I gave her a large brass bell to keep on her bedside table. If she needs us she's to ring it like mad."

"Do you think we'll hear it down here?" She was rather doubtful. The house was large, and swallowed sound.

"We'll hear it," he assured her. "I think they'll probably hear it in the next county. When I had measles she gave it to me, and she could hear it when she was in the paddock."

She looked up at him, amused. "Measles? When was that?"

He went red. "A couple of years ago."

"Measles?" she teased him. "That's a childish ailment."

His eyes narrowed on her face. "So it is, madam! I caught it late in life, and if you say another word about it I'll demonstrate just how childish I can be!"

Kate began to lay the table. He came, silently, and

took the knives and forks from her, and finished the job. She went back to her cooking.

"I spoke to Mrs. Butler about leaving," she said suddenly. "As soon as she's really well again, I'll find another job."

He didn't answer. She glanced round and found him watching her from beneath half-lowered lids. A frown curled his brow and his mouth was taut. They looked at each other in silence.

"You'll be glad to see me go," she half accused, half reproached him.

"I must be glad," he said flatly.

CHAPTER NINE

THE course of Mrs. Butler's illness did not run smooth. Her temperature ranged widely, her appetite varied from hour to hour, and she presented a puzzling picture to her doctor, who came each morning to check on her progress.

"It's this unpredictability which worries me," he told Kate with a frown. "She seems to swing wildly. One day I feel certain she's improving, the next she's much worse. I can't account for it."

Kate, too, was puzzled. Nursing Aunt Elaine, she too found the same peculiar variability. Gradually she began to suspect that the older woman was playing some sort of game, using her illness for her own ends. Yet, as soon as this thought had entered Kate's head, she was shamed by finding Mrs. Butler in a state of quite genuine collapse, her face white, her breathing difficult and pitiful to hear. When Kate summoned the doctor, he, too, showed signs of alarm.

"How long has she been like this?" He drew Kate to one side, out of earshot of the bed, but his eyes fixed on the fragile old face on the pillow.

"I just found her like it a little while ago. I went down to prepare her lunch. I was gone half an hour. When I came back she was lying there, half unconscious."

"How long has she been like this?" He repeated the words in a vague voice, frowning. "That's the thing that worries me. A pity you missed the point of change. If you'd seen a gradual change, or been here when she first collapsed, I might get a clue."

"A clue to what?"

"To what's causing these sudden collapses. Is she eating?"

Kate shook her head. She had been having great trouble in persuading Aunt Elaine to eat anything at all. "I wish I could talk her into eating a good meal, but she'll only pick at a few vegetables."

He frowned. "Vegetables? She needs protein to build her up again. Do you give her eggs? Fish?"

"I cook them, but she won't eat them."

He turned to stare at the figure lying so still against the pillows. "Why not? Doesn't she like them?"

"She was always a semi-vegetarian. She had a very small appetite before her illness—it has wasted away to nothing in the days since she first collapsed."

"We must re-awaken her appetite, then," he said firmly. "She must eat. This must be the answer—she's suffering from malnutrition. It would explain a number of symptoms which had been puzzling me."

Kate gestured with vigour. "I'll do anything I can, but how are we to get her to eat? I've tried my best. I've taken great pains with her meals, I assure you. I'm not a bad cook, and I try to make the food look really appetising. It seems to have no effect on her at all. She just pushes it away."

"Apathetic?" The doctor watched Kate keenly.

"Yes, that describes her attitude to food exactly."

He nodded. "Good. That sounds as if my diagnosis is pretty accurate. We'll use a mixture of science and magic . . ."

Kate looked startled. "Magic?"

He grinned at her with delight in his success at startling her. "Yes, magic—some people call it psychology, but I always think it has more in common with what witch doctors called their 'power'. We use our knowledge of the mind to cure people."

Kate laughed. "Using knowledge sounds pretty scientific, doesn't it?"

He shrugged. "Science is a more exact art. I'm going to have to use a mixture of guess work and intuition where Mrs. Butler is concerned. If I'm wrong, heaven help us." He pushed his hands into his pockets and rocked on his heels, studying Kate with laughing eyes. "At her next meal bring her the smallest portion you think you can prepare—a spoonful of fish, a boiled egg—tiny amounts. Put them on a big plate to make them look even smaller. Don't comment on their size. Just hand them to her. If she doesn't eat them, look sad. Go away slowly, give her wistful looks. Then at the next meal repeat the process. Once she actually eats everything you've brought her, you can begin to increase the amount—very, very slowly, a spoonful at a time. It may work."

Kate nodded. "I get the idea."

He wrote out a prescription. "At the same time, we'll give her extra doses of vitamins and iron—to build up her reserves. Together they should help. You need strength to face the daily strain of living when you are her age."

When Kate told Nick, later, what the doctor had said, he was amused despite his anxiety for his aunt. "Next time I'm ill I'll send for a witch doctor. It sounds a civilised way of being cured!"

Kate glanced at him, noticing with a pang that there were dark shadows beneath his eyes and a tightness around his mouth which had not always been there.

He had been sharing her watches in the night. They had taken turns in sitting up in case Aunt Elaine needed attention. She had insisted that Nick must go to work, although he had wanted to help Kate during the day, too. Had those difficult nights, followed by working days, worn him down, or was it some other strain which put the darkness into his eyes?

He was leaning against the wall in the kitchen, watching her blend a sauce, and the limpness with which he half reclined on one arm made her frown.

"Why don't you go and sit down for half an hour? Supper will keep."

"I'm starving," he retorted indignantly. "I thought it was almost ready!"

She looked at the sauce, dropping deliciously from her spoon. It would be a shame to ruin it, she thought. She shrugged. "Well, after supper, why not go to bed early?"

"Do I look that bad?" He pretended horror, peering at himself in a mirror on the wall, putting out his tongue at his reflection.

"Too much lost sleep, too little rest," Kate said firmly.

"Yes, miss, sorry, miss," he mumbled, giving her a glinting look from beneath half-lowered lashes.

She moved past him to get a sauceboat. He was so close that she could see the graining of his skin, the faint gold tips of his lashes, the faun-like folding of his ears.

She turned hurriedly away, her heart thumping. It was both pain and delight to be so near him.

Sylvia came visiting next day, bearing expensive, plastic-tasting grapes in a silver wicker basket tied with pink ribbons. She asked if she might go up to see Mrs. Butler and give them to her personally, and Kate uneasily said that she would see if Mrs. Butler was awake.

Mrs. Butler was reading, having gained a little in energy since the doctor's last visit. Kate had actually persuaded her to eat a small bowl of rice pudding that lunchtime, even though she had already eaten some plaice masked with a cheese sauce. The food had had some obvious effects. She looked up, smiling, as Kate entered her room.

When Kate told her about her visitor, however, the smile vanished, and a scowl replaced it.

"I will not have her coming up here! She's only come because she hopes I'm on my deathbed."

Kate looked shocked. "That isn't very nice!"

"I know Sylvia!"

Kate sighed. "I think you ought to see her."

"Give me one good reason!"

"For Nick's sake? She'll resent it if you don't, and she'll make Nick miserable for days."

Aunt Elaine sighed. "Oh, very well, you little blackmailer, bring her up. But don't leave us alone! I need support if she's to burden me with her presence!"

Sylvia was all smiles and sympathy, her slanting green eyes skimming everywhere, meanwhile. Kate busied herself with various domestic tasks while Sylvia sat on a chair beside the bed, despite Sylvia's irritated glances every now and then.

Aunt Elaine, out of a perverted sense of humour, sat up with a great display of health and vigour, talking in her old, determined way, her features irradiated by a flush which was born of anger rather than health.

Sylvia studied her carefully, assessing her state, and Kate saw the corners of the lovely, selfish mouth turn down as Aunt Elaine impressed Sylvia by her apparent strength.

Was Aunt Elaine right? Had Sylvia come out of a hope that she would be visiting a deathbed?

It would, of course, have been the perfect release from the fraught situation in which Sylvia found herself! Aunt Elaine would leave the battlefield for good, and Sylvia, without a blow struck, would be clear winner.

After ten minutes Sylvia left, obviously only too glad to go, and Kate ushered her out of the house. On the stairs Sylvia paused to look down into the hall.

"Dark and dingy! Needs white paint and that

front door replaced with a glass one—to let in light. All that old-fashioned hall furniture can go, too."

She darted away from Kate to peer into the rooms, exclaiming over the shortcomings of the decor and furnishing.

"Nick must give me a free hand. I'll give this house a new lease of life!" Her green eyes glowed feverishly as she hurried to and fro, examining, admiring, deprecating.

She had, Kate saw, a real passion for the house. In one sense Aunt Elaine misjudged her. Sylvia was as obsessively held by Sanctuary as Aunt Elaine herself—it was just that they saw the house differently. Aunt Elaine liked it in its present shabby, elegant state. She wanted no changes at Sanctuary. Sylvia had sweeping plans for changes here, but she, too, loved this house.

She paused to look at Kate with her face alight. "It has good bones," she said. "Don't you see it? You must see it. The house has been neglected. It's dirty and decaying, but underneath the dirt and the rubbish you can see the bones of a beautiful house."

Kate nodded slowly, recognising the justice of what Sylvia said. "I do see what you mean!"

Sylvia's features were alive with passion. "I must have it," she breathed hoarsely. "It's wicked what they've done to it—what's happening to it now. It could be the most elegant house in the county."

Kate remained silent. There was really nothing useful to say. Sylvia turned to look at her after a moment, her eyes narrowed in thought.

"That old woman upstairs," she said brutally, "how long do you think she'll live? I thought she might be dying this time. Nick seemed to be afraid she would. He hasn't been near me for days—he kept saying he couldn't leave her alone. I was sure she was really ill."

"She was," Kate protested. "Really ill! I was very worried about her, too."

"What did the doctor say?" Sylvia moved at once to the essential question.

"He was concerned, too. She was so weak."

"She doesn't look weak now," Sylvia said sullenly.

Kate was silent. She could hardly tell Sylvia the truth, that Aunt Elaine had been deliberately assuming a vigour she did not have in order to annoy her unwelcome visitor!

Sylvia looked at her searchingly. "Tell me the truth —is she going to pull through?"

Kate nodded. "I'm sure she will, this time."

The lovely face contorted with rage. "And then? Do you think she'll be as strong as she used to be? They always say that a few weeks in bed can be very weakening when you're old."

Kate was almost tempted to laugh, so blatant and childish was the selfishness and wicked dislike which Sylvia was displaying for her now. She swallowed down a chuckle, and answered with as much sober care as she could. "I think Aunt Elaine has a very strong will. If she wants to get well again, she will."

"And she isn't going to die and leave me in possession of Sanctuary if she can help it," Sylvia said astutely.

Kate half smiled, then sobered quickly as she met Sylvia's cool stare. "I wouldn't know about that."

"Oh, I think you have a pretty shrewd idea of the situation," Sylvia drawled. "You've been pretty lucky so far—Nick would have got rid of you at the start if he hadn't been a soft-hearted fool, and then the old lady got ill and made you indispensable. Odd, that, isn't it? Providential, one might say."

Kate gave her a wide-eyed look without answering. Sylvia glared at her.

"I suppose you think that the old lady is really fond of you? Nick certainly believes it." Sylvia smiled unpleasantly. "But I know better. The only thing in this world that matters to her is Sanctuary, and she would use any weapon to keep the house out of my hands. You're just a tool to her. If you had any pride you would find that distasteful. But you haven't any pride, have you? Just an instinct for finding a comfortable nest and settling down in it. Well, I'll put a stop to that. You can resign as soon as you like. If you don't, I'll save you the trouble!"

She turned on her heel and walked away, her blonde head held high. Kate watched her, drained of all emotion save a sick sense of disgust at the cruelty of which human beings are capable when self-interest dictates it.

It was not so much Sylvia's threat of getting rid of her that hurt. It was the idea that Aunt Elaine had merely used her as a tool.

And what of Nick? He, as much as herself, was merely the means to an end for Sylvia. Sylvia needed Nick if she was to possess Sanctuary. But did she love him? Kate had seen them together, seen Sylvia look at him with something of the acquisitive hunger with which she looked at the house. Was that all it was? Or did Sylvia in her own way love Nick?

In any case, Kate told herself firmly, it's none of my business. Nick and Sylvia must sort their own affairs out. I have to face the fact that I have no place here. Once Mrs. Butler is on her feet again I must go.

That afternoon she was scrubbing a piece of harness, which had been left untouched for years in a corner of the stable, when someone knocked loudly on the back door.

"Come in," she called, expecting a tradesman.

A small, slightly grubby face peered round the door and Kate stared in surprise. A boy of about eight inserted himself gradually, revealing an open-necked blue shirt and shabby blue jeans. Clutched to his small middle was a large hutch. Inside it a black and white rabbit sat, twitching nose and whiskers.

"Hallo," Kate said invitingly. "Who are you?"

"Kevin Nunn," the boy said hoarsely.

"Well, come on in and put your friend down," Kate told him in a friendly tone.

He stumbled across the floor and placed the hutch, with reverent care, on the floor.

"Will you give him a home?" He stood up, looking at her with pleading, desperate eyes.

"Why does he need one?" Kate asked.

"My mother had to go into hospital and my granny says she can't look after Robby as well as Dad and me. She said he must go. I thought you'd take him until Mum comes home again. I'll come back for him, honest!" He looked at her, lips trembling. His hand came out, at the same time. In the palm were clutched a handful of coins. "I brought money for his food. He doesn't eat much—he likes carrot and dandelions best."

Kate pushed his hand away. "Keep your money, Kevin. We have plenty of fresh vegetables in our garden. Bring Robby through into the stables and we'll pick out a nice warm place for his hutch."

He flushed with relief. "Thanks! I don't know what I'd do if I had to give him up for good."

He followed her through the garden to the stables. They decided on an empty stall which would give Robby fresh air and protection from the weather at the same time, and when Kevin had seen his pet safely installed, and fed him a small piece of bread and a few lettuce leaves, Kate offered to show him some of the other animals.

He was eager to see them. "Donkeys! You are lucky! I've always wanted a donkey. Robby was the first pet I was allowed to have—I've had a goldfish since Robby came, but the goldfish died. There wasn't much fun in him anyway. He just blew bubbles all day."

She laughed. "I know what you mean."

"Haven't you got any dogs?" he asked her, staring at the horses and donkeys with fascinated eyes.

"Yes, they're around somewhere. We let them run free inside the grounds."

"How many have you got?"

She told him about the dogs while he was stroking the donkeys. Patient and gentle, they let him come up close and finger their long ears. The horses nuzzled Kate, and Kevin laughed.

"Why are they pushing you like that?"

"They're looking for apple or sugar." She pulled out of her pocket a handful of sugar lumps, and handed them to Kevin. "Feed them these—they'll be your friends for life."

He looked a little nervously at the horses' teeth, and she showed him how to hold his palm flat beneath the loose-lipped animals' mouths.

Delicately, they snuffled up the sugar. The little boy giggled helplessly.

"It tickles! Can I give them some more?"

"No, one lump is enough. Too much is bad for them." She turned and saw the dogs streaking across the park. Kevin saw them, too, and gasped with excitement.

They met the dogs at the edge of the kitchen garden. Gambolling playfully, the three animals greeted Kevin with curiosity and noisy excitement. Kate glanced up at the house and saw Aunt Elaine staring out of a window. She had been drawn by the noise the dogs were making, and waved to Kate to bring the boy into the house.

Kevin was reluctant to leave his newfound friends, but he came upstairs to meet Aunt Elaine, when Kate explained to him that that was the lady who actually ran this delightful paradise for animal-lovers.

"So you have a refugee rabbit, have you?" Aunt Elaine said cheerfully, after Kate had explained his presence at Sanctuary.

He looked nervously at her, clearly half afraid that she would even now withdraw permission for Robby to stay here.

Aunt Elaine winked at him. "Do you know, Robby is my first rabbit? Mind you, there are plenty of wild rabbits in the park—we have to keep an eye on them, because they get into the vegetables if we don't watch out."

"You . . . you don't shoot them, do you?" he quavered, eyeing her with alarm.

She laughed. "Goodness, no! We just try to keep our garden fences properly wired. The foxes are their main enemy, I'm afraid."

"Foxes?" He stared, eyes like saucers. "Have you got foxes, too?"

"My dear boy, of course! Their dens are well hidden, but I've seen them in the twilight and the early morning, stalking rabbits and birds across the park. A flash of russet fur and they've gone."

Kate discreetly withdrew, leaving Kevin to sink on to the bed absentmindedly, drinking in every word Aunt Elaine said to him.

When she returned later she found them still engrossed in each other. She pointed out that it was getting rather late for Kevin to be out. He lived in the village, a walk of some fifteen minutes away, and his family would be anxious about him if he did not leave soon.

"I told Dad I'd come here," Kevin volunteered. "He said as how it was a chance, but he didn't think you'd be bothered with a rabbit."

When he had gone, Kate took Aunt Elaine a light tea; boiled egg with bread and butter, and a peeled banana with lemon jelly.

"Nursery tea, my dear?" She received a wry, affectionate glance.

Laughing, Kate sat down beside the bed. "I should have brought poor little Kevin some, too, then perhaps you would have eaten it!"

"Are you feeding me up, by any chance?" But Aunt Elaine began to eat her meal, despite her teasing.

"Did I tell you that Nick had showed me the cottage he's bought you?" Kate tried hard to sound casual. "It's rather a charming little place. It would be easy to run. It's been nicely modernised."

"I know the place," came the dry retort. "A neat little box for an old lady."

Kate glanced at her ruefully. "Nick is trying to please you, you know."

"Then he isn't succeeding! Look at this . . ." Aunt Elaine turned to pick up the silver basket of grapes which Sylvia had brought her. "Expensive, useless, idiotic! It sums up everything about the girl! She's not the person to take care of Sanctuary."

"Whoever Nick married might not be prepared to take on your animals!" Kate tried to make her protest gentle.

"The animals are irrelevant—the house itself is what matters. The house and Nick. Nick needs a warm-hearted, loving girl. He doesn't need Sylvia."

"Surely only Nick can decide that!"

She received a long, close look which made her flush hotly. "Nick knows very well that he's made a mistake. He needs to be helped to escape."

Kate got up stiffly. "I'll take your tray down if you've finished."

Aunt Elaine laughed softly. "Little ostrich!"

Kate did not care to think too deeply about the meaning of that enigmatic remark.

Nick arrived back early, ruffled and untidy after a day on a building site near London. He gave her a broad grin when he came into the kitchen, pushing back his hair from his forehead with the back of his hand.

"I must run up and wash before dinner! I'm a mess. I had a very tiring day."

"Sylvia came to see Aunt Elaine," she told him in a calm voice which she hoped did not betray any feelings either way.

"Oh?" Nick shot her a look. "I hope that that meeting went off all right?"

"They were polite to each other."

"No fireworks?"

"None that I noticed. Sylvia brought her some grapes and was very sympathetic about her illness." Kate tried not to sound ironic. If Nick had no idea how hopeful Sylvia had been, it was not her place to enlighten him.

"Good," Nick said absently, leaving the kitchen.

That evening, for the first time, Aunt Elaine needed no constant scrutiny. She lay reading for an hour or two, then switched out her light, so that when Kate peeped in at nine, there was only the deep steady sound of breathing in the quiet room.

Kate stood listening for a while, relieved and happy. Aunt Elaine was undoubtedly much improved. Her chest and cleared, her health seemed set fair.

She closed the door and slowly walked down the stairs, gradually falling into a melancholy mood. Now she must go. She had no further excuse for staying here. Aunt Elaine no longer needed her, and Nicholas wanted her to go.

She stood in the kitchen doorway, watching his bent dark head. He was reading, his profile turned towards her. He was wearing a pale blue sweater with a deep cowl neckline. It gave him a faintly monastic appearance. The strong chin and warm, firm mouth were relaxed, the dark hair slightly ruffled, curling a little against his neck.

He turned suddenly, sensing her presence. They looked at each other across the shadowy room. Nick smiled, involuntarily, with a tenderness that made Kate tremble and look away.

"I think I'll go to bed," she stammered. "Aunt Elaine is asleep now. She won't need anything else tonight. I'm sure she's really better now. Goodnight, Nick."

He answered absently, watching her as she fled in

disarray. His eyes narrowed, his lips tightened. For a long time he stared at the spot where she had stood.

Kate was surprised to find herself falling asleep quite quickly. She had expected to be wakeful for hours. Her thoughts were so painful and so confused that sleep should have eluded her. Her mind was a battlefield, yet her body, exhausted by many nights of sleepless care for Aunt Elaine, demanded that her restless mind give way.

She slept, yet her mind, having so far obeyed her body, was still unable to rest, and her sleep was disturbed by strange, chaotic dreams. Tangled images pursued her through avenues of darkness. Sylvia, offering her a silver basket of grapes, laughed spitefully and pushed her out of the gates of Sanctuary. Aunt Elaine tossed endlessly, flushed and feverish, crying out that she must not die or Sanctuary would fall into Sylvia's grasping hands. Nick looked up, his lashes masking his grey eyes, and Kate felt her heart drop sickeningly with passion.

She was back at home with her aunt in Devon. The sun was warm on her skin. Someone was knocking somewhere. She knew, vaguely, that it was Nick, and she cried out to him to let her go. She had to go, she told him.

Then she sat up suddenly, dream and sleep falling away. There had been a sound, something indefinable but alarming.

She listened, skin prickling. Again it came . . . it was the creak of a board. On the landing? No, she thought. She knew that sound. It was one of the boards in the hall.

Someone was downstairs, creeping along the hall.

Nick? She looked at the little clock on her bedside table. Nick, creeping about, at two in the morning?

She got out of bed, groping for her dressing-gown, and went quietly out on to the landing. She listened, but nothing moved. A clock ticked somewhere, a stately sound, familiar and comforting. There were no lights anywhere.

Slowly she tiptoed down the stairs. She was almost at the foot of them when she heard someone move in the hall. A clink, as of china, was followed by a strange rustling.

She peered down into the hall. There was someone moving about, a darker shadow in the shadows. Nick? No. Too short, too broad.

She moved to the light switch and clicked it down. Light sprang. The dark shadow swung, cursing in a startled, angry voice.

And Kate recognised him—the door-to-door salesman who had been so curious and importunate. He had been bending over the umbrella stand. On the floor near her lay a large holdall. It gaped, displaying some of the contents of the china cabinet; porcelain, silver, a few pieces of ivory.

As she looked at it the intruder ran at her, moving lightly for someone of his bulk. She was taken off guard and let out an instinctive shout. Then, summoning her wits, she screamed again, "Nick—help!"

Before she could scream again a large hand clamped down on her mouth. She was caught by the hair and flung backwards against the wall. Her head smashed against plaster with an impact that sickened her. She groaned and slumped to the floor, pain darkening her eyes.

CHAPTER TEN

FOR a while pain made her deaf and blind. Then, as the violent waves of agony subsided, becoming merely a steady throb, she began to hear again; a scuffling, voices, then a queer thud.

She pulled herself slowly up, clutching her head as a stab of pain shot through the back of her eyes. It was very hard to move, but she must make the effort. Slowly she prised her lids apart.

A figure blocked the kitchen doorway, looming like a tower against the light. Kate blinked, trying to focus.

It was Nick! He was beside her in a second, lifting her by her shoulders, his fingers moving over her absently as he spoke.

"What the hell did he do to you? Kate, are you all right?"

She had to speak, but it was an effort which hurt. "Burglar..." The word scratched out weakly. Her lips seemed numb with the barbed pain which was consuming her.

Nick shrugged her warning aside. "I've dealt with him—tied him up with washing line."

She giggled weakly, finding that funny for some reason. Her eyes were getting used to the light.

He gently turned her face towards him and swore

ferociously under his breath. "My God, your head . . . it's bleeding!"

"I'm only bruised," she assured him.

"Come into the kitchen. I'll take a look." Nick sounded brusque and icily angry.

"Police," she mumbled.

He nodded. "Yes. I'll go and ring them. Hang on here . . ." He left her. She leaned back against the wall, closing her eyes again with relief. It was wonderful to be back in darkness again.

Nick returned too soon. He gently guided her into the kitchen. Their intruder lay on the floor, neatly trussed hand and foot like a chicken. Kate stepped past him gingerly and he glared up at her.

"The police will be here in a few minutes," Nick told him cheerfully.

There was no answer. Nick made Kate sit down and brought a bowl of water over to the table. He tilted her chin, and she kept her eyes closed while he tenderly sponged her head.

"You're going to have a very nasty bump there," he told her. "It was bleeding, but it's not serious, just a graze. It's swelling already. Soon it will be all the colours of the rainbow."

When he had removed the water and dried her head, he glanced down at the burglar.

"I wish I'd hit you a damned sight harder! If you were not tied up I'd give you a good thrashing, you cowardly scoundrel! Anyone who can do this to a young girl . . ." Nicholas's voice broke off in frustrated fury and he glared impotently at the other man.

The police arrived shortly afterwards. They removed the burglar, took a statement from Nick and Kate and asked them both to come down to the police station later that morning.

The sergeant, a short burly man with a moustache, looked at Kate's bruised head, and advised Nick to call a doctor.

"She could have slight concussion. Head injuries are dodgy things. Best not to take any chances."

Nick nodded. "I'll do that."

The sergeant took away the bag of valuable objects which the man had been attempting to steal. "We need these for a while, I'm afraid—evidence, you know. You'll get them back in due time. We'll give you a receipt for them now. Could you make out an inventory?"

Nick looked through the objects and quickly scribbled out a list. The sergeant checked the list against the items in the bag, and signed it.

He left a few moments later, congratulating them both on their achievement.

Nick looked at Kate with a rueful grin. "It's you we have to thank. I only just heard you screaming my name. I didn't hear the burglar at all. If it hadn't been for you we would have lost all that stuff."

"I heard him moving about," she explained.

"I seem to be piling up an enormous debt to you," he said. "How shall I ever repay you?"

Kate looked down at her fingers, twisting them into a knot. She could not think of anything to say to him. Huskily, she stammered, "Nonsense . . . anyone would have done the same . . ." Then, with a flushed face and feverish eyes, "I don't want your gratitude!"

He put a slim hand over her contorting fingers and gently straightened them. "What do you want, Kate?" His tone was strangely tense.

She swallowed, her pulses drumming, and did not answer him. After a moment of taut silence he stood up and moved away from her. "I'd better ring the doctor."

"No," she said in quick protest. "Not in the middle of the night! I'll see him in the morning when he comes to see Aunt Elaine. I'm certain I haven't got concussion."

Nick hesitated, then agreed. They put out the lights and went back up to their beds in silence.

Next morning Kate was washing up when suddenly remembered that the burglar had been studying the umbrella stand when she switched on the light last night.

He had seemed interested in it when he last came. Could it possibly be more valuable than Aunt Elaine imagined?

She mentioned it to her when she took her some hot milk later that morning, but Aunt Elaine laughed and shook her head. "Why, of course that thing isn't valuable! How could it be? Victorian mass-produced at its ugliest?"

"I like it," said Kate.

Aunt Elaine looked at her with tender amusement. "Well, if it's going to worry you, by all means call in an expert. Try the phone book—look up Pan's Cellar, an antique shop on the road to Malden. The owner is a retired don, knows a lot about these things. He can come out and give us an estimate of the value."

Kate rang the shop before Aunt Elaine could change her mind, and the owner, his voice coolly interested by the name of the house, promised to call that afternoon.

The doctor was late that day. His arrival coincided with that of the antique dealer, so Kate asked the doctor to find his own way upstairs, and took the dealer down the hall to look at the umbrella stand.

She explained the circumstances of the burglary of the previous evening, and the man listened thoughtfully while he examined the stand from all angles. He seemed particularly interested in the base and the interior.

"Could I take this into some lighter room?" He stood up, holding it carefully.

Kate showed him into the drawing-room. He gave a curious look at the contents of the room, then concentrated on the umbrella stand for a long while.

Kate watched him eagerly. At last he seemed satisfied, and looked up at her, slipping his magnifying glass into his waistcoat pocket.

He was a thin, tall man with thin greying hair which strayed down over a bony forehead. His pale blue eyes were intelligent but cold. The fine nose and mouth gave him a poetic delicacy of expression, but Kate was not sure she liked him.

"You're an observant young lady," he told her.

"Know anything about antiques?"

She shook her head. "I'm afraid not."

"Then you've been very lucky. This is sixteenth-century Chinese and quite valuable." His voice was still unruffled, quite cool. He showed no signs of excitement.

"Mrs. Butler thought it might be Victorian," Kate volunteered in delight. It was wonderful to have been proved right.

"There were many Victorian imitations—earlier than that, too. Our own manufacturers copied the Chinese stuff which we had imported earlier. They were very fashionable during the eighteenth century. But this one . . ." he touched the long vase with a careful finger, "this is the genuine article."

"It's a miracle it survived," Kate breathed.

"It undoubtedly is," he agreed, "after being used as an umbrella stand! Now, what is Mrs. Butler going to do with it? Sell it? I could handle that for her. I think I have a buyer—American, very wealthy. She would get a fair price."

Kate smiled at him. "I'll have to consult her first. I don't think she's really considered the possibility of the vase being valuable."

When she went upstairs she found the doctor still talking to Mrs. Butler, discussing the weather and the agricultural prospects for the coming summer. The early spring, he felt, might prove a calamity later.

Aunt Elaine at once asked him to inspect Kate's bump, which he did gently, assuring them after a moment that it was not serious.

"Painful, though, eh?" He touched Kate's cheek with one finger. "Brave girl! I'm afraid I can do nothing for you. The bump will go down in time. For the present take aspirins if your head aches, but not too many. They only lead to tummy trouble later."

When the doctor had gone Kate told Aunt Elaine the good news about the umbrella stand. Her excitement blazed as she spoke, and the other woman smiled as she listened.

"Nick must be consulted about this, of course. It's his vase, after all."

"Of course!" Kate flushed. "I'd forgotten that!"

She went back downstairs and told the antique dealer that the owner would be in touch with him if his services were further required. They had agreed to pay him a fee for his evaluation of the Chinese vase, but he now said that he would waive it for the time being.

"I will take it out of my commission if you permit me to sell the vase," he told Kate.

Nick arrived home half an hour later, to drive Kate to the police station to make a further statement. When she excitedly burst out with the news about the umbrella stand, Nick was bewildered for a few moments.

"What Chinese vase? Umbrella stand . . . do you mean the one in the hall, that old Victorian pot thing?"

"It's sixteenth-century Chinese," Kate assured him with a glowing face. "I suspected that the burglar was very interested in it, so Aunt Elaine let me bring an antique dealer here to check it. He wants to sell it to an American, Nick. He says it's very valuable."

Nick stared at her in astonishment. "Does he, indeed? You have been busy, haven't you, Kate? Nursing Aunt Elaine, saving us from burglars, looking after the animals. And now this! Busy, busy Kate!"

She flushed a bright, burning red and looked away, terrified that the tears would spring to her eyes and betray her. His tone had stung, sardonic and mocking as it had been, and she wondered angrily why he should taunt her in this half-malicious fashion. What had she done to make him look at her in that strange way, his eyes derisive, his mouth curling in a sharp smile.

"Well, I shall have to find somewhere else to be busy soon, shan't I?" She forced herself to reply in a light tone, pinning a false, bright smile to her face. "I mean to start looking for a new job tomorrow. Aunt Elaine no longer needs me. I've done all I can for her."

"For us all," Nick drawled in the same odd voice. "So you're moving on, Kate? We shall miss you." He did not sound as if he meant a word of it.

They drove to the police station, leaving Mrs. Pepper to guard the house and Aunt Elaine, and were ushered into a waiting-room. When they had read the posters on the walls, skimmed through some dog-eared magazines and fidgeted on their chairs for about twenty minutes, they were taken off to separate interview rooms to make their statements. They left some hours later, weary and fed up.

"Bureaucracy!" Nick spat the word out angrily as he headed for Sanctuary. "The world won't end with a bang—it will just suffocate beneath its own weight in official forms! Everything in triplicate! The same questions over and over again!"

"They were very polite and helpful," Kate said faintly. "They brought me two cups of tea, and biscuits."

He blazed, "Thank you, Pollyanna! That was all I needed, sweet and holy comment from you! Sylvia's right about you and Aunt Elaine—one has to defend oneself against you both."

"You don't need defences against me, Nick," she said in a cold voice.

His rage had died, though. He glanced at her sidelong, his mouth pulling down at the corners. "God, I'm sorry, Kate. That was unforgivable of me. I'm a brute. It's the strain. . . ." His voice faded and the firm mouth clamped together. He said nothing else for some time.

Then he asked her, "Have you spoken to Aunt Elaine about leaving Sanctuary?"

"Yes," she admitted.

"What effect did you have?"

She sighed. "I'm sorry . . ."

"She wouldn't even consider it?" He spoke tersely, his frown heavy.

"When she's just been very ill, possibly more ill than we realise, how could I press the point? She thinks of the house as her home, Nick! To leave Sanctuary might kill her!"

"Do you think I haven't thought about that?" He turned a dark, tormented face towards her. "Don't mention the idea to her again. I've changed my mind."

She was very still, afraid to look at him. In a thin, still voice she asked him, "Changed your mind, Nick?"

"I can't ask Aunt Elaine to leave her home. She's too old. Sylvia . . . we must come to terms with the situation as it is."

What would Sylvia make of that? Kate wondered. She shot Nick a pitying look. He was driving with a set expression, his knuckles white on the wheel, his jaw clenched as if to control some fierce emotion which threatened to overwhelm him.

After a moment he said huskily, "Kate, wait a while before you look elsewhere for a job. Aunt Elaine still needs you." He paused, then added tersely, "We all need you."

CHAPTER ELEVEN

SYLVIA'S party was crowned with success from the start. She had had her wish, and the weather was fine. A clear, unclouded evening sky was sprinkled with a few faint stars. A crescent moon rode the horizon like a slice of thin lemon. The wind was mild and warm, from the south, and the barbecue could be held safely in the paddock next to her house.

Her family were solid middle-class. Her house, a square, modern building in red brick with a neat garden and unimaginative decorations, was perhaps one reason for her obsessive desire for Sanctuary. Sylvia undoubtedly saw the elegant, decaying old house in a very favourable light after the rather boring comfort of her own home.

She had never lacked money, and Kate guessed tonight that money was really not as important to her as the ownership of Sanctuary. Money could not buy you everything.

Sylvia hung on Nick's arm tonight, glittering and deadly, like a silver snake, her slender body curving towards him, her blonde hair fanning his dark shoulder.

She wore a very tight silver dress which was ridiculous for a barbecue yet somehow looked superb in the pale light of the lamps set up around the paddock.

Kate observed that Sylvia was careful not to walk far. She stayed within the ambience of the tables set up for the party, her small silver-clad feet unmuddied by the paddock since she walked always on the boards laid down to surround the cooking and serving area.

The air was blue with smoke and fragrant with the odour of cooking steak, and the subtle tang of the herbs which were being sprinkled on the meat as it cooked. Marjoram, rosemary and thyme gave a pungent savour to the meat.

Kate, innocent about barbecues, had come in slacks and a warm sweater, expecting a casual party. Many others, she was glad to find, had done the same. Sylvia stood out among them all like a firefly among midges. She moved, shining and charismatic, among her guests, followed by many pairs of eyes; some admiring, some envious, some resentful.

Nick arrived at Kate's elbow, handed her a paper cup. "Sorry, no glasses, because it might be dangerous if one was broken out here in the dark."

She thanked him and sipped. The flavour was odd, warm and spicy.

"Hot punch," Nick said with an amused grin. "Well, it's supposed to be hot. What do you think of it?"

"Very pleasant," she said.

Sylvia tinkled up to them, her arm curving up into Nick's elbow, her hand white in the darkness. Thin silver bracelets clinked as she moved. She wore earrings which matched.

"Nick, our guests want to talk to you!" She ignored Kate. Her smile at Nick had the quality of ice shimmering under the rising sun. There was a veiled threat to her words.

A band had arrived, a few young musicians in sequin-studded costumes, carrying instruments. Figures moved to and fro, switching on the electricity which powered the electric guitars.

When they began to play, the guests stood about, applauding, then began to dance. The ground was dry enough to be used for dancing, and the paddock had been mowed carefully the previous day. A scent of new-mown grass still hung faintly in the air.

Nick was dancing with Sylvia, his dark head bent over her fair one, her slender body glittering in his arms.

Kate watched them with bitter pain, then looked away hurriedly as Nick glanced across at her.

Nearby she caught a glimpse of the distinguished stranger she had seen several times with Sylvia, Sir Rodney Paton. He, too, was watching Sylvia and Nick. He had a rueful look about him as he stared at them.

Kate watched him, pitying him and wondering what it was that men saw in Sylvia that could hold them so irresistibly. She was very beautiful, it was true, but she was cold and selfish. Were men unable to see the truth about her, or did they prefer to shut their eyes to it?

Suddenly Sir Rodney turned his head, as if becoming conscious of her scrutiny, and looked at her. Their eyes met, and Kate blushed. He smiled, quizzically, and walked towards her.

"May I have this dance?" He had a quiet, warm voice which she rather liked.

She hesitated for a moment, uncertain of her response, but she had little choice, unless she was prepared to be uncivil, and so she smiled back and thanked him.

He danced extremely well. At these close quarters she found him even more attractive than she had expected. He was not a young man, of course, but he had been very handsome, she saw, and still retained a faded aura of good looks. There was charm in his smile; in the twinkling eyes and well-cut mouth. He was confident, relaxed and easy to talk to.

He asked her about herself, was interested when he heard that she was employed at Sanctuary. She caught his quick glance at Nick, saw a shrewdness in his good-humoured face as he assessed Nick briefly.

"How do you get on with Mrs. Butler?" The question had a faint amusement behind it, and she suspected that he had heard Sylvia's version of the relations existing between herself and Mrs. Butler, and that he had not necessarily believed it wholesale.

"I'm very fond of her," Kate said frankly. "She's been kind to me, and she has a warm heart."

"An animal-lover, isn't she? Prefers animals to humans?" He looked down into Kate's face with a quirk of his eyebrows, inviting her to respond with amusement.

"She loves animals," Kate agreed. "But she loves her nephew, too—more than the animals, I'm certain."

"Ah?" Sir Rodney was interested. "Yet she opposes his engagement? A possessive woman?"

Kate shook her head. "That's not her reason."

He watched her face thoughtfully. "Do you know why she opposes it, then?"

Kate hesitated, then looked up at him, her eyes clear and cool. "It really isn't my business, Sir Rodney."

"Quite right," he agreed softly.

They circled for a while, passing Sylvia and Nick. Sylvia looked at them with a faint frown, her expression haughty. Nick glanced at them, then did a double take, his brows jerking together. Kate blushed under his fierce scrutiny, and looked away, trembling slightly.

Sir Rodney looked down at her curiously, then looked at Nick. The two men stared at each other intently.

Sir Rodney whistled softly under his breath, a little smile curling his mouth.

Jimmy Whitney was standing beside the barbecue tables, holding a jacket potato in a paper napkin. He waved and grinned at Kate as she walked towards him with Sir Rodney.

"A friend of yours?" Sir Rodney studied him. "I've seen him before, I think."

She introduced them. Jimmy was polite but non-committal. He put down his baked potato and asked

Kate to dance, wiping his fingers neatly on another napkin.

She shyly excused herself to Sir Rodney, and slid off with Jimmy, his arm around her waist. The music softened to a waltz. There were fewer couples on the paddock. Many people had moved off to sample the food.

"I've bought a new car," Jimmy informed her with great satisfaction.

"Another one?" She laughed up at him, her eyes warmly teasing. "How do you afford it? Does your father mind the way you keep spending all your money on new cars?"

"I have to have some pleasures," he said rather sulkily. She saw that her suspicion had shot home. His father had complained to him about the number of new cars he kept buying.

"I suppose it's a fairly innocent hobby," she comforted. They whirled around in silence for a while, wrapped in a friendly mood. Jimmy looked down at her to smile, his nose crinkling in a teasing look.

"Why not come and have a look at my car? I'll take you for a test drive. It can do a hundred miles an hour. I've had it out on the motorway—the London road. It was a fantastic sensation. The power seems to throb under your feet."

She shivered. "Thank you, Jimmy, but I'm afraid speed like that terrifies me. I prefer my feet on the ground."

"Coward," he scoffed. "Come on, I dare you!"

They flew round in a graceful swirl. She caught

Nick's glance as they passed him, and wished suddenly that she was wearing more feminine clothes; a full skirt which could flare elegantly when she danced like this. Nick's brows were lifted in a cold derision. His lip twisted slightly, in a faint sneer, as though he were inwardly laughing at her. She felt a pulsing fury in her veins as he turned his head to smile at Sylvia, so lovely and deadly in her silver gown.

"Well, if you want me to come for a drive, Jimmy," she said impulsively, "I'll come!"

He grinned at her in delight. "Great! We'll have a drive along the lanes for half an hour—there's never any traffic on these roads at this time of night—too isolated. We should be able to try the car out in all her paces."

She had a sudden qualm. "Not too fast, Jimmy!"

He smiled at her calmingly. "Of course not, you goose!"

As they walked out of the paddock gate they bumped into Sir Rodney, leaning thoughtfully against an elm tree whose shade made him almost indistinguishable. He leaned towards Kate, smiling curiously. The flare of the electric lights gave his face a look of returned youth.

"Not leaving, I hope?"

"Just for a while," Jimmy told him lightly.

"I look forward to your return," he said with a little bow of courtly courtesy.

Jimmy grinned down at Kate as they walked towards where his car was parked. "How did you get to know the great Sir Rodney? He's quite an old card, isn't he? Very attentive to the ladies, I've heard."

"He just asked me to dance earlier. I only met him then for the first time." She stared as they halted beside a gleaming little sports car, all shiny chrome and scarlet paint. "Good lord!" Her tone was awed.

"Isn't she fantastic?" Jimmy touched the bonnet with a proprietorial finger. "Hop in—and I'll put her through her paces."

The air rushed past them at an alarming speed as he put his foot down on the accelerator. Kate gasped a warning. He grinned, and slowed down to take a corner. Dark green hedges, the far, misty levels of the marshland on the horizon, and above them the sky, clear and soft, starlit and hauntingly lovely. Her skin glowed with the rough caress of the wind. Her hair blew back, tangled in dozens of curls; flying out over her shoulders.

The bright beam of their advance preceded them along the lanes. Now and then they passed small cottages, whitewashed and set in neat gardens. Once they saw a Victorian villa, bay-windowed and massive, set about with laurels and monkey puzzle trees, their shadows thrown upon the old brick walls by the light of an antique lamp set in the gateway to illumine the path.

The roads were narrow, without pavements, hemmed in by hedges. Fields pressed up towards them. A few elms, dotted here and there, with the occasional coppice of hazel and birch, broke the flat level of the land.

Jimmy drove with an intent expression, engrossed in his thoughts. Kate lay back against the seat, dreaming. Nick's face swam up towards her, his mouth tender, his eyes gentle. Her lips parted on a sigh. She closed her eyes in melancholy pleasure.

Then suddenly light blared, music broke up her mood. They were back at the barbecue, having travelled in a circle. The paddock was ablaze with lamps. The amplifier throbbed to the bass drum. Guitars strummed. There was a steady twitter of voices above it all, and the clink of plates.

"Look at that," Jimmy said, climbing out of the driver's seat, and coming round to help her out. "They're eating all the food! We just got back in time!"

Kate was half reluctant to return to the noise of the party. The drive had been soothing, relaxing, and she wished it could have gone on for ever. She smiled at Jimmy, thanking him. "It was a wonderful drive!"

He was exultant. Leaning down, he kissed her on her mouth, his hands lightly holding her shoulders.

Then he released her and turned, almost falling over Nick. Jimmy looked startled, then grinned unashamedly. "Oh, hallo there, Nick! Fancy finding you in the middle of the lane!"

"Where the hell have you been?" Nick's voice was stretched taut with a rage that made him dangerous. Even in this light Kate could see the menace in his eyes and mouth.

"We went for a spin. Any reason why not?" Jimmy flung the challenge jauntily.

"Yes, Nick," a cold, icily contained voice drawled from the paddock gate, "let's all hear the reason!"

Nick stood very still for a second, then turned slowly on his heel and looked across the shadowy lane at Sylvia. She was leaning on the gate, sinuous and dazzling in the flare from the lamps behind her, her tight dress moulding her slender figure. Her lovely face was frozen with anger. Her eyes spat hostility. Her mouth was thinned and tightly held at the corners.

Beside her, lounging and watchful, Sir Rodney was a patient observer. His iron-grey hair was smooth above half-amused, half-eager eyes.

"Well, Nick?" Sylvia repeated. Nick was still silent. His hands were clenched at his sides. His shoulders were rigid with his attempt at self-control.

Jimmy laughed aloud and slid an arm round Kate's waist. "Nick was playing the heavy father again. Come on, sweetie, let's mingle with the crowd."

Nick watched them pass him without a movement, but a muscle jerked at the corner of his mouth, betraying him, and his very rigidity of posture was as clear as any action.

Sylvia walked slowly across to him. In a clear, hard voice she said, "I'm sorry, Nick. It would never have worked, would it? I'm not prepared to wait for your aunt to die, and she would never give in, either. We might as well call it quits."

He stared down at her, without moving or replying. She held out her engagement ring. It sparkled in the light, a cold, colourless stone. Nick gestured silently to her to keep it.

"I'm going to marry Rodney," Sylvia went on coolly. "He hasn't got any aunts."

She turned on her heel and walked towards Sir Rodney. He took her hand in both of his, raised it and kissed the knuckles, then slid a ring on to the third finger. The stone in it was enormous, a glittering sapphire. Sylvia looked at it, then raised her mouth to him briefly for a sealing kiss.

Jimmy and Kate had watched the incident from the gate. Jimmy bowed to Sylvia, mocking and amused. "Congratulations, Princess. A tug of my forelock to you." Then to Sir Rodney, in a quiet voice, "You'll be marrying the most beautiful girl this side of London, sir, but she needs a tight rein. I'm an expert on fillies. Take my advice."

"Damned insolence!" Sylvia flared furiously.

Sir Rodney gave Jimmy a long, curious look. "Could you be envious, young man? Would you like to be the one with the tight rein? Or am I misreading the situation?"

Jimmy flushed and moved away hurriedly. Sylvia laughed, her slanting eyes widening in triumphant amusement. She gave her new fiancé a stroke of the cheek, her fingers caressing. "Darling, you're so clever! Poor Jimmy!"

Kate watched them move away in total disbelief. That Sylvia should have cut the Gordian knot so decisively, of her own accord! She could hardly believe it!

But what about Nick? He had said nothing, done nothing. He still stood in the shadowy lane, where he had stood all this time, his face enigmatic. What was he thinking? Had Sylvia hurt him, after all? Kate had begun to believe that Nick was no longer in love with Sylvia. She had begun to think that . . . She broke off the thought in a shiver of anguish.

"Come here," Nick called in a soft, taunting voice.

She stared at him across the lane. Behind her the music throbbed, the lights blazed, the people danced and chattered. Nick stood in the darkness, his back to the hedge. It was hawthorn, breaking into fluttery white blossoms which showered down at every wind like fragile confetti, making the grass gay with summer.

A few white petals floated down now, some lingering on Nick's dark hair. Kate walked slowly towards him, giggling a little at the sight.

"What's funny?" He caught her wrists and drew her back, out of sight of the paddock, into the darkest corner of the lane.

"You have hawthorn flowers in your hair," she said huskily, wondering if he could hear the pounding of her heart.

"If I ever catch you with Jimmy Whitney again I'll punch his nose for him," Nick returned, ignoring her remark.

"Why shouldn't I be with Jimmy?"

His hands slid from her wrists to her shoulders. She looked up at him, melting and wide-eyed, her tangled hair brushing his fingers. Nick half glared at her, his jaw set.

"You know perfectly well why! You must never

go out with anyone but me!" His face descended towards her. Hungrily their mouths met, her hands slipped up his chest, clung to him.

Kate did not know if she could bear the joy which consumed her. All pain and doubt fell away, as though it had never been, and she glowed in incandescent happiness.

Later, his mouth against her ear, he whispered, "From the first moment I knew you were dangerous, even in that dreadful shabby old coat. You had such a trusting, gentle face. It made me want to pick you up and rush off with you. I was furious with myself, with you, with fate."

"I knew you were angry with me," she murmured. "You so often were!"

"What else could I do? You were so lovely, and I was already tied to Sylvia! I had no choice but to fight my feelings for you!"

She nodded. "I know! Sylvia had the right to expect that you would keep your word and marry her!"

He groaned. "Sylvia came along at the moment when I was just beginning to want to settle down. I wanted a home, a wife, and children. She was very beautiful and she obviously liked the idea of marrying me. I'd never been in love before—I mixed up love and desire. I wanted Sylvia because she was so beautiful and exciting. I thought it was love. Then you came along, shy and shabby and unbelievably adorable, and I was shaken alive. I realised then that I didn't, never had, loved Sylvia. I was in love with you . . ." He groaned again, brushing her neck with his lips. "If you knew how much!"

"Darling," she whispered joyfully, clinging to him.

"Once I knew how I felt I was in torment. I had no right to stop you dating Jimmy, yet I wanted to kill him for looking at you. I had no right to kiss you, but I couldn't stop myself. My only defence was to stay away from you, feed my anger. I tried to ignore you, I tried to forget my feelings, but it just made things worse. I was out of my mind just now, when Sylvia finally released me. Thank God she did! We would have led an intolerable life together."

"Sir Rodney will give her everything she wants," Kate said. She was sorry for Sylvia. She suspected she had felt far more for Nick than he had for her.

Nick led her towards his car. "Come on, let's go and tell Aunt Elaine. She'll be almost as happy as I am. She planned this from the very start . . ." Kate opened her lips, but he put a finger against them gently. "Don't protest, my darling. I know she did! She saw you as her ally against Sylvia at first, but very rapidly she guessed how much I was attracted to you, and she threw us together as much as she possibly could! She's a cunning, devious, unscrupulous woman—and I love her very much. I'll be grateful to her for the rest of my life."

"I hope you don't think I was a willing party to her plan?" Kate asked uneasily. "Once I realised what she was hoping for, I wanted to go. I would have gone had she not been ill!"

Nick gave her a sideways grin. "My darling Kate,

you're far too transparent to be a successful conspirator. I read your thoughts pretty clearly."

"Oh, did you?" She was indignant.

He laughed in triumphant glee. "Ah, that stung, did it? Did you think I was unaware of your response when I kissed you that evening? That I was blind to the way you were beginning to feel? I knew I could make you love me. That was why I hated you to see Jimmy. You were so young and inexperienced. I wanted to be the one to awaken you to womanhood."

She gave him a cross, half piqued look. "Vanity! I'm not that easy to read!"

"Aren't you?" His eyes were mocking. "Well, perhaps I was being a little optimistic, but can you put your hand on your heart and tell me that you didn't have any idea of what it was between us?" His smile was arrogantly demanding. "Well? Tell me you didn't suspect I found you maddeningly attractive!"

She blushed and smiled, shaking her head in silence.

The grey eyes sparked. "You knew damned well how I felt—I gave myself away a thousand times. Why else did you go out with Jimmy, curse him? It was a deliberate tease for me!"

"No!" Her head came up, her colour high. "It was nothing of the kind! I admit, I did it partly because you were so set against the idea . . ."

He laughed cynically. "There you are!"

"I was defying you out of a sense of pride, not to make you jealous!" She gave him a long, serious look. "I resented being ordered not to see him! You had no right to do so, after all. I was your employee, but my private life was my own."

"And with any other girl it would have remained so," he agreed. "It must have seemed strange to you that I should be dead set against Jimmy! Of course I had no right to interfere in your private life. My specious arguments were just a cover. I had to hide the truth from you. But I think you guessed, all the same."

"No," she protested. "I thought you loved Sylvia . . ."

He bent his head and kissed her passionately. "Sylvia was a mirage—when the vision vanished I saw you, real and far more beautiful in your shabby coat, because you had the intelligence and sensitivity she lacks, and I could read your heart in those clear brown eyes of yours. You have such warm, loving eyes, Kate. They smile when your mouth smiles. It was only after I'd seen the miracle of your smile that I realised that Sylvia's eyes never smile. Her mouth moves, but her eyes remain icy."

They drove back to Sanctuary in a contented silence. Kate lay back against the seat, watching Nicholas's profile with half-closed eyes. She felt tired but happy, and achingly alive.

The moon swam over the roof of the old house, trailing a thin glitter of stars behind it across the purple sky. The trees stood in that pale light like black fingers reaching upwards to pull down the moon. Over the lake moonlight spilled in shimmering white pools, reflecting trees and house and stars. A white horse moved out of the shadows to stare at them, then dropped its head again incuriously.

They parked behind the house and walked through the garden to the kitchen door.

The lights were on. Nick grimaced. "Mrs. Pepper should have gone home by now—or is it Aunt Elaine disobeying doctor's orders to creep downstairs?"

When they entered the room they found Aunt Elaine, her white plaits hanging down in schoolgirl fashion, wrapped in a dressing-gown, nursing a lamb on her lap. She looked round at them half defiantly, half sheepishly. "His mother died," she mumbled. "I said we would rear him. Mrs. McTavish at Crumbles Farm has two others to rear, and hand-feeding takes so long. What else could I do?"

"What else, indeed?" Nicholas sounded grimly amused. "I think I shall definitely change the name of this house to Animal Farm!"

Then Aunt Elaine took in their linked hands. She looked at them in sharp question, hope dawning in her eyes.

Nick grinned at her. She gently put the lamb into the cardboard box she had prepared for it beside the fenced-in range, and came to them, holding out her thin, veined hands with the eagerness of an excited child.

"Oh, my dears! Nick . . . Kate . . . my prayers have come true . . ."

Nick kissed her cheek, shaking her gently by the shoulder as he looked down at her. "Prayers are one thing, Aunt Elaine—but interference is another! You didn't just pray, did you?"

"God helps those who help themselves," she said, her long nose and straight mouth full of pride and content.

"You wicked old woman," Nick scolded.

She hugged Kate, who smiled helplessly at her, brown eyes full of dreams. Aunt Elaine took Kate's hand and placed it back in Nick's grasp, patting the entwined hands with a smile of great self-congratulation. Then she looked from one to the other with curious eyes. "But what about Sylvia?"

"Sylvia told me tonight that she's going to marry Rodney Paton," Nick said cheerfully. "She very sensibly saved all of us from an impossible situation."

"Humph!" The vivid blue eyes flashed in irritation.

"Now, be fair," Nick shook his head. "I could hardly break the engagement, could I?"

"Old-fashioned attitude!" snorted Aunt Elaine. "Victorian principles!"

"Perhaps," he said coolly. "Nevertheless, I had asked her to marry me. It would have been humiliating for her if I broke the engagement. I had to let her do it."

"And if she hadn't?" Aunt Elaine demanded.

"I was pretty certain she would, eventually," he shrugged. "I was using you as my trump card. Sylvia would never have married me while you were at Sanctuary. Once she saw that you were going to be a permanent fixture here, she dropped me. As she so bluntly said, Sir Rodney has no aunts."

Aunt Elaine laughed delightedly. "So I do have my uses! I'm glad my tactics were the right ones."

"They were disgraceful," he informed her sternly. "You and your animals and your pretty orphan secretary . . ."

"I do wish you wouldn't call me an orphan," Kate said with some indignation. "I'm no more an orphan than you are! We neither of us have any parents, after all."

"Ah," he said wickedly, "but I don't have big innocent brown eyes and a helpless, appealing smile . . ."

She glared up at him, but with a glinting look in his eyes he slid his hand around her waist and pulled her closer. "Let me go," she protested.

"Once aboard the lugger and the girl is mine," he whispered, kissing her beneath her ear. "You have been warned! I've got you now, and I shall shut you up in my castle for ever!" His light mocking tone only just hid the passion which lay beneath.

"Sanctuary isn't a castle," she retorted. "It's a refuge!" She looked around the kitchen with dancing, bubbling joy, looking at the geraniums, the bright china and the warmth and gaiety of the whole room. "Especially this room—the heart of the house . . ."

Nick looked down at her, his unguarded heart in his eyes, those eyes which had seemed so cold to her when they first met. "You are the heart of the house," he said huskily.